D0628607

The Flight
of the
White Crow

Rachael Ann Mare

Spunky Misfit Girl
PO Box 4363
Sunnyside, NY 11104

ISBN-13: 978-0692728987
ISBN-10: 0692728988

For all the spunky misfits:
May you escape your must-dos
and find your proper place
in the human world

First, before all, Kaa must know: There is nothing, for us, but our right and true sacred duty. We live for this, and only this, one thing-to-do.

It is simple. It is right. It is shek; shek is law.

It is this: There is, on one side, a world of humans. There is, on the other, a dark place where souls keep until time is no more. We live in the in-between, knowing both.

Human-souls, when their selves of the world no longer move, must fly to the dark place. But they do not always way-find well. They lose the path. Their young-years pull them to remain.

Thus we, the Murder of the Kaa, must show them. We must guide them from one life to the next. We are soul-ferriers, and nothing more.

It is our truth. It is our way. It is shek.

First, before all, Kaa must know this.

~from The Aw'aw'aw, Most-High Book of the Blessed Ways of Shek

CHAPTER ONE

What the crow-girl Fannilea was about to do was not the right and true thing.

It was alone. It was different. It was not the will of the Murder. It was not all together.

It was against shek—against their way. Against what was meant to be *her* way.

How could she? They would say. *Not good, they would caw. Against your people. Stop, stop.*

But something inside of her begged her to do it—had begged her, for ever long, to do it. She couldn't name it, that feel. It was two things at once—a fear creator, but also a movement maker. It called to her. *Looksee!* it said. *Here is another way. A different way. A better? way ...*

It called to her, louder than the dark voice of her people said *Safe in the Ahk is the way.*

Yes, here in the Ahk was safety, maybe. Ahk, the nest, the home. The place of belonging. Here, her whole life planned. Here, knowing who she was. Shek, the way. Her life's work—to follow it.

Here, that was all.

Out there? Some sparkle-brightness, maybe. Some way to follow that thing inside, begging. She had kept it there since youth, trying to be of her people, but keeping on wondering. Of late, she had planned. She had waited. She had readied.

Now the time had come.

One gnarly-bent tree grew here in the Ahk nest. Perched near the top, she angled herself off a thin branch, claws clinging, dipping out over space, muscles snappy-sharp. Her half-ruined left wing hung crooked, but that would be no stopping-block. She had taught herself to live—and fly—with it as well as any Kaa; she had had no other choice.

The crow-girl trembled. She had power and she had fear, and she did not know which was stronger.

If they caught her, would they kill her? Throw her in the erawk, that much was certain. She would not let them do that to her again. But neither could she stay in this empty-of-life place.

The Murder lay beneath her, dead to the world, totaled by makeberry juice. Black-feathered bodies littered the pebbled ground, motionless like lumps of charcoal, burnt up and sooty. Tonight they would not stop her. Tonight she would use the thought of their laid-out crow selves as fuel for the flight ahead. She would leave them there, useless things, and start new.

Different. Alone.

This was one chance; there might not be another. The Murder broke free of rules only by order of shek—once per human year cycle, a part of the ritual Aug festival. The rest of the time, they were always checking checking checking.

One human-month, the Aug was. A feel of burst-apart, like fireworks, bubbled beneath her skin, and the only thing stopping it was the plan she kept close to her feathered breast. She had joined the festival, as she must. Ate alk'aw, she had, though it tasted of dust and gritted like sand in the beak (what else would you expect from bread made by dead souls?). Sang that kekked song of fealty again and again and again—so much singing! And read passages from the most-high book of the blessed ways of shek. Done it all, she had, like a good member of the Murder.

Even the worst, she had done, been able to do, because of her heart's plan. Thinking of it got her through the not-flying.

Not-flying was the worst.

Flap, ascend, buoyment, soardom, far above … flying was the only thing like itself. It was the best thing about being Kaa. It was her favorite.

But the Aug festival forbade it, and obey the law she had, no matter how hard it was. Now the Aug had, after a feeling of so long, come to an end. The Kaa had tossed out the last of the alk'aw and turned to their joyful festival-ending meal of makeberries. Through the human-month of the festival, the makeberries hung on the bushes and fermented, and after that their special juice enslaved the Kaa to more-more-more desires. One makeberry at the Aug's end made them eat eat eat.

They stuffed their bellies full. They sang and flapped and celebrated until they fell over like the dead, wherever they were in the moment the makeberry-fuzz took them. There they would lie, not stirring, until more hours from now.

For the crow-girl Fannilea, the smell had been the hardest. After a month of choking on alk'aw, stopping herself from drinking down the makeberries was not what she wanted. It needed much strength. Tartness burst around her as the Murder snapped berries in their beaks. Juice flowed over tongues, down the sides of beaks, and onto breast feathers.

Taste the tang, she almost could—oh how she had wanted it! Oh how she had felt it in her feather-points and claw-tips.

But not eating was the only way to escape.

So she had blinked her desire back and snapped her beak to resist. The others thought she was snapping up berries and berries, more berries.

It was not as hard to fool them as she had worried.

Thank her feathers for that, for Fannilea was not like her crow-family. She was not black-feathered. Against the dark wings of the Murder, Fannilea shone white. Sometimes, when she was crow in the human world, and she stood in the sunlight at just the right angle, at just the right time, her feathers glowed, iridescent. The light danced against them as though catching the shimmer of a layer of silver dust.

The Murder did not like it.

Fannilea knew she should not like it either. She should want black-featheredness, like the others. Shek said, *There is no room for ones. Only all.*

But Fannilea could not deny her secret pride. Her white feathers gleamed, and they were *beautiful*, and they were hers. She did not want to be ashamed.

Tonight, she did not have to be. For those white feathers had saved her. They had made the working of her plan. They had given her this moment.

On ebony feathers, makeberry juice cannot be seen; it disappears. A black-feathered Kaa may drink up and mash down as many makeberries as she pleases, and a stain will never show. She might be sticky, but the Murder would not *see*.

But on clean white feathers, makeberry juice drips down the breast in slim pathways, and then, as one rivulet joins another, morphs into an uneven, spreading patch. It seeps into the feathers and more, bleeds into the layer of down beneath. Deep there, it will hold fast for days and days after that crow-girl indulges, a mark of her difference.

But tonight, Fannilea had not indulged. She snapped her beak, waddled with feigned tipsiness, and hopped with only partially pretended merriment.

Instead of drinking and eating for true, she smashed berries against her chest, throwing her head, letting the stain spread, letting it brand her as a part-doer in this, her final Aug festival—even as she fizzed with glee at her coming soon goodbye.

Drunk themselves, the Murder believed.

Too caught up, they let her be and passed out flat.

A flash of pride she had for this, a successful plan—though shek forbade that, too. *Pride makes us ugly.*

But she must wait no longer; it was time to go. She spread her tail feathers.

Down below, a wing fluttered.

Fannilea's crow-heart leapt.

A beady eye opened.

Kek. She had dallied too long. Someone was awake.

"Fannilea?"

Nestling mate and crow-brother Corley, he of the white-tipped feathers, cranked his head up to pinchy-peer at her.

Surely Corley would not betray her. They had grown up together.

"Doing what, sister-crow?"

She did not answer.

Corley struggled against makeberry-fuzz. He scrabbled, wings flailing, claws scritching. But he could get no purchase; his limbs were weak.

"Cannot go," he whispered.

Cannot go.

Yes, she argued. *Yes, go.*

Alarm reflected in his eyes, and she could see that he would not keep quiet. Corley opened his beak.

Fannilea, balanced against her crooked wing, unleashed the other. Flapping hard, she launched from the branch, her beak pointed in the direction of her ultimate goal: the human world.

CHAPTER TWO

Fannilea flew.

More than on her physical strength or endurance, she called upon her heart. She reached deep within, beyond her crow-heart, to the human one that lay behind, and she called upon it to make her strong and fast and undaunted.

She put her beak into the stale air of the Ahk and flapped against it. She tried not to curse that kekking broken wing, but to balance against it and use it as best she could, as she had taught herself.

The right thing, it is not. Against shek.

The gray light swarmed; it fell like a great weight upon her back. Kek, how she struggled to leave it behind! She closed her eyes against it and used her other senses to keep her direction true.

Her crow-heart beat hard with exertion; her human-heart filled with worry. Would the Murder wake to Corley's summons? Could they be after her even now?

She risked a turn of her head for a peek behind her. The sky stretched gray, empty. Were they back there somewhere, out of sight?

She saw nothing.

She flew harder.

Against shek.

It would not take long to reach the border. Once she slipped into the human world, it would be less easy for them to find her. If she could only get there.

How she wished Corley had not woken!

Then she heard it.

Aw aw rawk bra bra —

13

That kekking song. It would kill her.

It is you. It is your blood. Listen.

Clear and shimmer-true, crow-strong, the tenor voice that sang to her echoed familiar in her heart.

Corley.

Fannilea had never been much of a singer, but Corley … Corley had a voice that glittered and danced and charmed the ears. It made Fannilea want to drop everything to sit in place and listen.

Corley sang the driving beat of the Het Ket Wok Aw Aw, but in his bell tones, the notes rang shiny-sweet. They fell soft as down, and she drank them up.

Bra bra aw alk aw

Life-rhythm, it is. We are. Together. Shek is.

Everything.

Fannilea's crow-heart wavered.

Her shoulders drooped, the weight of wanting to turn back drawing them down. The song had a power unmatched. The magic spell of a lifelong lesson—the only life she knew.

She ought to go back. What was she doing here, away from her crow-family? They were her people. She should be with them. Alone was not right. How had this happened?

Fannilea's crooked wing drooped, and she wobbled. As she shifted her focus to righting herself, the song fell away, and she was of her own mind again.

She must not let him get to her.

She must not let *them* get to her.

She opened her beak and sang. Her voice could not match Corley's for sweetness, but she had a set of lungs built for volume. The only real song she knew was the Het Ket Wok Aw Aw, but she wouldn't let that stop her. She made up her own song, a note-jangle beat-down hop-to-it tune, and belted it out as lusty as her lungs allowed.

The border was near; it spurred her on. Pounding heart(s). Flapping wings. Singing singing singing as she flew, until—

The wind stole her breath.

Wind?

Without warning, the air changed. No longer stale and dead, it whipped her face, chill and brisk. A misty rain damped her feathers, but it bothered her not.

Weather! She had made it—the human world at last.

Here you will not be you. Here you will not belong.

She opened her eyes. Here the sky hung black as crow feathers, but twinkling stars and wafting gray clouds revealed a tapestry of change. Here, nothing stayed still for long. It was the world of the living, and the living *moved*.

Fannilea's crow-heart fluttered.

Here she came alive.

Here she could breathe.

Here she could break her fast with more than makeberries! French fries for breakfast … Oh how she loved that just-right food!

Her joy drooped, tempered by fear. Corley's song followed her still. She didn't hear other voices; he must have come alone. The others had not woken, then.

That was something. Maybe.

Fannilea kept up her loud rawking and flew.

In the distance, she saw light. Would he follow her to the city? He hated it so.

She spied a dot, here, there, three, more, and then, with one more flap of wings, a golden haze sloshed over the horizon. The night receded for miles, beaten back by a dazzling light-patchwork.

She flew toward it. The wild life of them, it was, shining there. What a change from the nest she'd come from. Would she be able to find a home here?

No. Go back.

Her crow-heart thumped, and the sharp, chilly wind —surely it was the wind—stung tears into her eyes.

Her half-ruined left wing ached, hollowlike. Her hearts wailed; her senses strained. But the shining city buoyed her, and Fannilea soared. *Rawk rawk*, she shouted at the straight, sky-reaching towers.

She didn't know how it would be for her there, but this busy new place fascinated her. She wanted to know it. She wanted to be part of it.

She had seen it only once before, as a nestling. A messy place, it was, this thing the city. Running this way and that, full of all different kinds—even ones who didn't make sense in the life they started with, who had to make their own. Ones like her, maybe.

Corley's voice rang out behind her, strong with melody, but the sight of the city below urged her forward. The wind blew brisk and wild, and she shivered, but kept on.

She dove into the lights.

The singing stopped.

Wok? Fannilea cranked her head around, listening. The wind rattled.

No song.

Had Corley given up? Would he leave her be?

It did not mean the Murder would. They would seek her. But it was a big city—with many places to hide.

For tonight at least, it seemed she was free.

Fannilea whoop-cawed and dove again, honing in on the southeastern part of the city.

Roost-place, she needed. Treetop, her crow-family would say. But no. A rooftop for her.

Nature knocked down trees. But human buildings stood through rain, wind, and wildness. they stood even through earth-shudders.

Fannilea scouted the buildings below, searching for not-quite. Not-quite centered. Not-quite lived in. Not-quite busy, but not-quite silent. Some nesty place she could adopt, as her own, where no one would ...

There. In the middle, with the red brick and boarded-up windows.

She glided closer. Leaf-color caught her eye. One flap, and there, a garden-place—with a potted bamboo tree, paint-peel park bench, pebbly fountain, and growy-herb glass domes. Something there, on the bench. Feathers?

She dropped out of the sky and perched on a bench arm. A pink carnation twined with the wrought iron. And on the seat, a human face-covering—a mask—made from white feathers. Almost like it called to her, like she belonged to stay here.

But someone lived there. She should not stay. Not-safe, it would be, if they found her.

The white feathers of the mask fluttered in the wind, and she couldn't shake the stay feel. She was tired. Tomorrow, at day rising, she would new-place hunt. Only some few hours it would be, now, for rest. And here … so nestlike!

She plumped her feathers, glanced round and round, and then, predator-safe, buried her beak in her chest.

Still she listened. That song … would it start?

But it was absent. Not a song in hearing. The world held still, the sleepish city slow and quiet and resting.

Fannilea fluttered inside with worry yet. How to sleep? The Murder must be on its way, singing or no.

But her long flight and the escape tension took hold. Her eyes slipped shut, and her mind wandered sideways into sleep.

CHAPTER THREE

Fannilea awoke to the chill of cold metal against her temple. She did not open her eyes.

Traffic rushed below, and a cold-slatted bench pressed against the arm she lay on. The rooftop, she remembered. But something was different ...

Her temple. Her arm.

She was human.

Kek it all. She had changed in the night.

Her breathing quickened, and her hearts whirred with fear. She had stayed on someone else's rooftop, and now she was human instead of bird. Kek and twice the kekking kek.

"Stand up, girl," a voice said. It was male, without any soft feel, cold like the metal against her head.

Fannilea flicked one eye open.

The face matched the voice—hard lines and flinty strength. Light tan cheekbones, thin and high as the city skyline, and eyes of steel gray that offered no quarter gave him the look of a serious fighter, protecting his nest. But he was a boy, barely more than a year older than she. How curious that someone so young should be so full of iron. And self-regard—a keeping of himself to himself.

Pride makes us ugly.

Fannilea wanted to ask him things.

But there was a gun.

She ought to take care.

"Up," he said again. "The hands up, too." He stood, keeping the gun pointed at her, and backed up a pace.

She obeyed him, slow, so he could see, no trouble.

"Where did you come from? How did you get up here?"

Fannilea croaked. Kek. Out of practice. She cleared her throat.

"Leave, I must. I will. I mean—I will leave. I do not mean harm."

He did not waver. "Answer the question."

Fannilea yanked a hand through her hair, short, spiky, white like her feathers. He would not believe the truth. But she did not have anything else.

"I flew."

Mockery twisted his upper lip.

The world stopped, and something in Fannilea whuzzed alive. Everything centered on that cruel mouth of his.

It was the first emotion he'd shown, and she wanted him to turn it on her. A dare in disguise: Don't challenge me; you will fail. But he was wrong.

She could win.

Beat him, she could.

It made her wild with a song of fire.

Her crow-heart fluttered, and her stomach echoed it.

She twitched and tried to look normal. Human-normal, she reminded herself.

"And … why are you wearing … that?"

Fannilea glanced down at her shroud. Made of rough black cotton, it hung on her wiry frame like a sack. Kek. Her heart-plan had included a right-clothes step, before people-finding. But maybe she should thank the Morrigan that her people's ways-magic included *some* body-cover.

A blush rose in her cheeks.

"Are you on drugs?" He sprang, grabbed her wrist. Yanking her arm up, he inspected her forearm.

The nerves in her right arm tingled, and the damaged ones in her left arm answered back.

Glaring, she pulled away. *Drugs* she didn't know, but the not-rightness showed in the set of that mouth. Make him let her go, she would. He asked too many questions. She had to find a home! And much to do before people-talking.

She opened her mouth to explain.

A great clatter set up on the other side of the roof. Then a shout.

"Slate? Slate, what are you doing?"

A girl shoved up behind the gray-eyed boy.

Nothing but eyes and hair and black, that girl. Saucer eyes and nesty hair, and everything else was tiny bones, draped in black. She had purple streaks in chunky bangs. Furry black cat coat, holey-black wool leg covers, stompy boots like a weapon. Next to the iron-boy, the girl had a face like a brand-new cheepy chickie, unguarded.

"She isn't answering me."

The cheepy chickie-face disappeared, swallowed by a voice like a mama lion.

"Ohmygod, put that gun down! She's a girl! She's barely wearing clothing!" The girl marched between Fannilea and the gun.

"She can't stay," Slate said to the chickie-lion girl, lowering the weapon.

"Oh for bull's pizzle," the girl said. "You're already worried about *that*?"

"I will leave," Fannilea said, sideways-look-stealing at the edge of the roof. She didn't want to get caught between these two.

The girl pinched the short sleeve of Fannilea's shroud between two fingers and sniffed.

"In this thing? Definitely not. Maybe you didn't notice, but it's *winter*. You'll freeze to death. Ice-boy here might be okay with that, but I'm not. Come inside. I'll find you some clothes."

"Keep an eye on her," Slate said. "And don't tell her about the house. She's not staying." He turned and crossed the roof.

Anger warbled in Fannilea's throat. She had told him she wanted to leave! She didn't want to stay in his half-made nest; why did he have to be so kekking pig-headed about it?

The chickie-lion girl sniffed. "Sorry about him," she said, at a volume that carried. "He's like a little guard dog with a Napoleon complex—he snaps at everything. But don't worry—he doesn't bite."

Slate threw open the access door. "*Cabrona*," he said under his breath. Then he got louder: "If she causes trouble, I'm not helping you."

In return, under her breath, the girl said, "Yessir, whatever you say sir, Master Commander, sir."

As the door swung shut behind him, she said, "Don't listen to him. If you need a place to stay, stay. There's plenty of room, and we'll talk him into it."

"But—" Fannilea glanced again at the edge of the roof. She could change to crow and fly off.

Kaa do not change in front of humans, only lost souls.

Left that behind, she had. But she didn't like it, same still. Living here, rightlike, would mean way-finding as one of them. As they did.

"No arguments," the girl said. "You need clothes." Her gaze caught on the white-feathered face-thing. "Is this yours?" she asked curiously, picking it up.

"No," Fannilea said. "Not yours?"

"No," the girl said. "I wonder where it came from."

Shrugging, she strapped the elastic over her head. The mask turned her into a halfish crow-girl, and a tingly-sharp feel scuttled along Fannilea's spine. The girl gripped her arm. Steered them both toward the door, she did. Strong, and more dangerous, maybe, for not showing it like the iron-boy, this chickie-lion girl. Tricky. Fannilea should get away, fast as can be. No matter what she felt. It would be safer.

"While we're at it, I'll tell you about the house. Who knows? Maybe you'll want to think about becoming an official member."

Fannilea shivered, but not from cold. Didn't humans live not-like Kaa? No Murders. But what was this? Official member, nothing. Fannilea wanted to be free. No more shek. Had she flown straight from one Murder into another?

CHAPTER FOUR

We wake.

A great raucous series of *aws* and *woks* and *kets* shatter the peace of the Ahk.

Our crow-daughter is missing.

The white-feathered one, Manak's foster-thing, the one he took in when no one wanted her. Trouble.

Saying her name displeases us. We don't know why, but whys don't concern us.

Beneath the noise runs a current, an uncawed one, but one that belongs to us all—perhaps we ought be glad of it. That crow-girl never belonged.

But shek will not have it. She is one of us. She must be brought back. It is not a matter of our will, but of our way.

"Quiet!" a voice booms, and we fall silent, as we know we must.

Awoah Datchett Ata Hearn perches at the top of our tree and surveys his flock. Our able leader has forward-turned shoulders, a barrel chest, and reed legs. He maintains these characteristics in human form; therefore humans find him unassuming. But they must also find him powerful and persuasive, no? For him to fulfill shek and do his job and lead well, yes. They must find him charming, even. And so for that, in Datchett's head, crow or human, burn two fire-bright black eyes that unveil souls—eyes that hint at mischief and invite the deepest darkest parts of whatever they look on to rise to the surface. If you gaze into those eyes, you will see a deep desire to be good—yet also a welcoming empathy for the occasional foray into the wicked. For who among us is perfect? We are all wicked some of the time.

Datchett Ata Hearn is a good awoah, and he will bring that wayward white-feathered thing into line. Datchett tells us of these things in his lilting way of speaking, and we understand.

(Of course no one will mention the time she was thrown in the erawk and came out more fighty-bitey than ever, not shek-right and yes-sirring as she ought.)

(Of course no one will mention the riik she led, that couldn't-be-right riik she had tried to weasel out of, the pop of her wing—no, we will not mention that.)

(Most especially of course, no one will mention the one who is said to have escaped the Murder, long ago. Kaa do not dwell in the past.)

We have a right leader, and he will tell us what to do.

"You must hush, my dear Murder," Datchett says, though the lone voice disturbing the Ahk is his. A gentle reminder—we are safe in his hands. As long as we obey. Reassurance, it is.

"As you all know, for we are bound, one of our flock, our white-feathered crow-daughter, called Fannilea

Ishika Fiachra, has disappeared in the wake of the Aug. A terrible, treacherous action, to take advantage of our celebratory state, but we must not lay fierce blame or give way to hate, for she is one of us, a blood-bound Kaa, and it is not for us to judge her, but to bring her back to the fold of the Murder and show her the right path. That is what we shall do, for we are her family. We are her people."

At this, we cheer. For it is the true thing, and it is good. Good of our awoah to steer us right, toward love-inclusion and away from anger-shunning. For the white-feathered crow-girl belongs to us. She is us.

A cry keens from amid the flock.

"How will we do it, Datchett? Lead us!"

The crier is Corley Drust Fiachra, he of the white-tipped feathers. Isn't he nestling-mate and helper crow-brother to the white-feathered one? Didn't they play together as little birds? Should we wonder about him? But Corley is a good Kaa. He follows shek true. Not like his sister-crow. And isn't he showing enthusiasm for her recapture? There can be no question; he has the right path. Despite his unusual feathers.

Datchett, being wise, knows these things, too, for he stretches his beak to Corley, encouraging.

"You must not panic, my flock. You will feel it greatly in your hearts that the Murder has been rent apart; of course you will. It is indeed a great sadness, but you must not let it drag-drop you. It is only a thing to challenge and change us. It is only a thing we must work through—we will mend the Murder, and we will be stronger for it."

We cheer. If any crow notices that Datchett has not exactly answered young Corley's question, of course not a one mentions it. Datchett is the awoah. Ours is to listen and obey.

"Darlings. We will need strength. Not only what strength we know we have, but that which we are not aware of—our deepest reserve. As such, after much consideration, I have chosen to call in someone who can remind us of that strength. Dear flock, I believe we can count on the utmost support of the Morrigan."

Silence falls.

Our leader is wise. Our leader is capable. He knows what is best for us.

But … to call in the Morrigan? Is that not drastic?

A fearsome creature, beast and goddess, the Morrigan can appear as a raven-haired, buxom beauty who hides a mouth full of razor-sharp teeth; or as a dark-headed man armored for battle, brandishing keen-edged weapons; or as a great raven itself, as natural and birdlike as those you see in the human world, until it turns its head and fixes its too-knowing eyes on you; or even as a night-hound with burning red eyes and a wide, slavering jaw. She most often chooses the woman; she waits until it pleases her to show the teeth. This is the way she, like Datchett, most often gets what she wants.

The Morrigan holds sway over war, feuds, and hatred—all things violent. She chooses who lives and who dies in battle, and she likes nothing more than to stir things up for her own amusement.

Is this a battle? Is the Morrigan needed? No one questions our capable awoah, to whom we are steadfastly loyal, but nothing hangs more terrible over us than the Morrigan.

Into the quiet, Datchett sounds the call.

We cower.

Our white-feathered crow-daughter is worse-deep than we thought. With the Morrigan involved, it will not—it *cannot*—go well for her.

A storm cloud rolls in on the horizon. Deep purple sky roils above and below, threatening thunder and rain. Amid the turmoil rides the lady Morrigan, flanked by two large, mean-eyed ravens. Her dark hair blows wild around her head, one violent white stripe bold among its waves. Lightning streaks electric behind her. She smiles upon us, gently, showing no teeth, and we stare back in awe, except Datchett, who stands tall and proud at the front of us, awaiting her.

The clouds bear her to the pebbled ground, and she glides off and bows.

"Datchett," she says. "What a pleasant surprise. You called for me?"

Neither Kaa nor human, yet all language she speaks and understands. It is a not-comfortable feeling. She is a thing apart.

Datchett hops closer.

The ravens at her shoulders follow his hops, hostile-eyed, but the Morrigan bends down and stretches out her hand. Datchett walks into it, and she raises him close to her face so he may speak.

He uses dulcet whispers.

It is not like our awoah to exclude us. But it is not ours to question. We let him do what he must.

The Morrigan returns him to the ground and addresses us herself.

"Your awoah has informed me that you have an escapee. He has full confidence in your ability to recapture her on your own, but he has graciously requested my involvement because he thought I might enjoy the opportunity. He's right; I would. You may have no doubt that I will set your wayward girl straight, though my methods may seem to you circuitous. You must know that your awoah and I will stop at nothing to keep the Murder together. Wayward Kaa will not be tolerated. You have called upon the Morrigan, and you may be certain she will come to your aid. Have no fear—Fannilea Ishika Fiachra will be dealt with as she deserves."

A small but firm voice calls out.

"But, Morrigan. Where is she? What is she doing? How will we find her?"

The white-tipped brother-bird again. Daring to speak directly to the Morrigan.

Corley holds her look. He does not seem heart-worn for his own safety. Could it be he worries for the white-feathered girl?

The Morrigan bends down, searching. We lean away, not liking to get too close to those teeth. But one among us stands straight, and that again is Corley the white-tipped one. He waits, and she gazes into his eyes, and still he does not flinch.

"Corley, is it?" the Morrigan asks. "The white-feathered one's brother-helper? You mustn't worry, son. I know where she is."

A gasp goes up among us.

A slow smile spreads across the Morrigan's lips, revealing those iron-spike teeth. We shudder, and she smiles wider.

"Of course I do! Am I not the goddess of life and death? Am I not charged with the care of you all? You must let her be for now. She will set up her own end.

Bide your time. Have faith. When I need you, I shall call on you. Until then, you must live your shek."

With that, and a thunderous clap and a flicker of lightning, the Morrigan and her ravens disappear.

The Ahk is gray and silent as before, except for a few hushed and worried whisperings.

CHAPTER FIVE

The chickie-lion girl led Fannilea into the house.

Its insides were half-broken. Plaster lay in clumps. Paint peeled. Electric wires hung out of sockets. Graffiti covered walls.

"Be careful on the top floors," the girl said. "We use the basement for storage. The first and second floors are in good shape. We've been here for a year. We each spend a few hours a week working on the house."

Fannilea cringed. More shek.

On the second level, at the end of a long hallway, the girl pushed through a fire-engine-red door. "Lemmee see what I have." She stuck her human-beak in the closet and plucked at clothes. "I'm Leaf," she called over her shoulder. "We mostly go by nicknames. Nobody wants to be the same person they were before. Easier that way."

The room put Fannilea in mind of a dream. With walls the color of clouds before rain, an old-fashioned perch-place for making words, red window-feathers hanging helter-skelter and tangled with a soft white vine of lights, a pretty, pretty place it was. Best of all, a fluffy white nest of pillows cozied one corner.

"Is that where you sleep?" Fannilea asked, pointing at the pillows. "In the nest?"

Leaf came out of the closet with a pile of black in her hands. "I guess it is like a nest, isn't it?" She studied Fannilea with crinkled edges round her eyes. "What's your name, then?"

Fannilea hesitated. Should she? She wasn't going to stay. But ... the girl made her want to. Those liquid-saucer eyes. That funny nesty hair. This room … how safe it seemed. Was it a trick?

She would be on her way soon, though, and living in their world meant being humanlike. They would expect her name.

"I am Fannilea Ishika Fiachra."

"Wow," Leaf said. "That's some name. What if we call you Fann?"

The crow-girl had never had a nickname. A glee-shudder swept across her shoulder blades.

"So you sleep here … apart?" she asked.

"This is my room, yes," Leaf said. "The one next door is in decent shape if you want it."

"My … room?"

All belongs to all. Mine for none makes peace for all.

Fannilea … Fann had never owned anything of her own, to herself. In the Ahk, she hadn't even had her own branch. In the human world, she had shared everything with her nest-mates and crow-family, Corley and Manak.

Leaf held out the pile of clothes. "Only if you want. Here, see if these will fit."

Fannilea struggled into the clothes—black jeans, black tank top, big black sweatshirt. A black-feathered human, she became.

"Not perfect, but it'll do," Leaf said, giving her a once-over. "That's how it is around here. Make do with whatchya got."

Time to go, then. But … there was something Fannilea had to know. "Did you make the garden?"

"Yeah, I did! You like it? I want to add a trellis. And some ivy! More flowers! The others think it's a waste. 'We already have a backyard.' But I like being high up. Plus, less chance the neighbors will see! Want to help? We could—"

"No, I must go."

"You have somewhere to stay?"

Fannilea dodged the girl's gaze.

"Where will you go?"

She didn't know, but better that than a new Murder.

"I'll be all right."

"You should stay."

Fannilea quick-looked toward the window, her shoulders rustling with unease.

"We're all orphans here. Some by choice. Others by necessity. Doesn't look like much, but it works."

Fannilea wished she could explain. But she didn't know how to translate shek. "I ... don't like groups. I don't ... I don't like make-you-do."

"Make-you-do? Like stuff you have to do? Nobody likes that, do they?"

Fannilea struggled. "Worse. Among my people ... it is ... right make-you-do. Blood-right. Without choice. You must. You will. You do. It is, and that's all."

She had been barely fledged when Manak started her lessons. So many times she had asked, "But *why*?" After many stumble-nothings and stutter-wonders, Manak finally said, sternly, that it just *is*.

Fannilea did not do well with just *is*. She could not put her questions away. Not without answers.

"But you're here," Leaf said. "You must have chosen something different."

Slowly, Fannilea said, "Yes. Here I am."

"Your people ... who are they? Were you in a cult or something?"

"Cult? I ... don't know this."

"A group that ... sucks away your life."

"Yes," Fannilea said. "A cult. You are right-thinking."

"Did something happen? Were they ... hurting you? Should we call the police?"

"No police," Fannilea said hurriedly. "I am OK. Only heart-hurts. Please, I ... don't like to talk about it."

Leaf blushed. "Of course. I'm sorry. I talk too much. No more questions, I promise. But you could stay for breakfast. We have eggs."

"No, I must go." Fannilea's human-heart jangled with not-like. But she could not risk to stay. Even for breakfast. She would get sucked in.

"At least let me send some things with you." Leaf pulled a tote from the closet. "Food, and a blanket."

"I don't—"

"No arguments," Leaf said. "You'll need it."

In the kitchen, Leaf filled the bag to the brim with food. She stuffed a small blanket on top.

"Are you sure you don't want to stay?"

Safelike, it was, in a Murder. You did not have to figure out what to do. You did not have to decide. You obeyed. Someone else took care of all.

Fannilea remembered her moment, atop the tree in the Ahk, ready to soar. In a Murder, you could not do this. You could not change what you did not like, and you could not find the things you did. Stuck, you were.

"I am sure," she said.

CHAPTER SIX

Corley Drust Fiachra had been summoned.

He shiver-shook with fears, but obey he must. It was shek. He would go.

He followed his instructions: Fly to the end of the Ahk. Even when you think you are done, fly more. There, a tunnel opens beneath your claws. Follow it down. Follow follow follow. When reaching the end of the tunnel, go no farther. Wait.

When he reached the end of the tunnel, Corley came into a room of wide space with arches up up and up. The top disappeared before he could make it out. Dank stone formed the walls, but bumps stopped the smoothness. Something not-right about those bumps. Eye holes, maybe they had. Nare holes, too. Like crow skulls. Corley averted his eyes.

In front of him stood a plain wood perch.

A wide, tall chair carved of black stone towered over the perch, turning it tiny by comparison.

Ugliness chomped at Corley's crow-heart as he settled on the perch. This room, he did not like. That chair, he did not like.

Not-nice-for-sits, it looked. No cushy part. Straight and square. A vine twisted there, at the back, with thorn-spines growing. When a person sat, the points would prick. But then, it wasn't a person who would sit, was it?

Worse, the carvings. Corley stretched his neck and saw human faces, hurting. Mouths with screams. Cheeks clenched. Eyes of agony. Was the stone moving? Were the faces …?

Corley clacked his beak and wrenched his neck back. His crow-heart thumped. He did not know how long she made him wait; he tried not to mind. He hummed the Het Ket Wok Aw Aw to calm his heart.

A mist formed slowly, hanging. A heavy gray curtain fell between Corley and the throne. He shifted his claws, but remained on the perch, waiting.

The mist flowed toward the throne and coalesced into the shape of the Morrigan, calmly seated, in her aspect of woman. A black dress revealed her milk-white neck and shoulders; raven-feather sleeves began at her shoulders and cascaded down her arms. A black diadem crowned her black tresses with the one white stripe. Rich purple dusted her eyelids, while kohl outlined their shape. On her lips she wore black paint and a bemused smile, no teeth.

Her ravens flew in from somewhere behind her and perched on either side of the throne.

"Corley," she said. "Thank you for coming."

Corley bowed.

"The white-feathered girl, the one who escaped, she is your nestling-sister?"

"Wok. My father raised her from a one-day-old."

"And you wish to see her returned to the Murder?"

"Wok. I do, greatly."

"Does your sister listen to you, Corley?"

"Aw?"

"If you asked something of her, would she comply?"

Corley blinked. Kek. Of course Fannilea would not do what he asked of her. She was not a good crow-sister. Bitey-fighty, she was, even as a nestling. Smaller than he, but stubborn. Pluckish. He had not always won their fights. Even when he had, it did not mean she did what she ought.

"Depends," he said.

Would the Morrigan condemn his crow-sister? She had behaved so badly.

But the witch only nodded gravely.

"You've done your best to deal with her, haven't you? But she's not easy to have as a sister."

"Not so, no."

"Causes a lot of trouble."

"Wok."

"But not you. You obey your Murder."

Funny-sounding, her voice was. Displeased? It could not be so. Corley behaved.

"Wok."

"If I asked you to go and tell your sister that I'd like to see her, do you think she would come?"

Corley whuffed. Why couldn't he have a normal crow-sister? One like his friend Wrede, quiet and concerned with shek and nothing else. Instead his days —his life—went away with worrying about and being sent to fetch that crow-brat Fannilea.

But that was not sheklike. Hadn't he and his crow-sister played up-high true-joy flying games? Wrede did not enjoy games. Not much new-think in her crow-brain. Not like Fannilea.

But they were too grown-up for games now. Corley would have to fetch his crow-sister. Again.

"Wok. I believe she would."

"'I believe she would,'" the Morrigan mimicked. "Oh for Badb's sake! If you don't know, say you don't know. I'm sending you. I want to meet with her. Talk her into it."

Corley ruffled his feathers.

"Be my messenger," the Morrigan said, with a must-do voice-tone. "And I will help return her to you."

Corley eyeballed the Morrigan. He did not trust the witch. Up to something, she must be. Tricky goddess.

But she was the right law of his people. Awoah of the awoah, or something like. Shek said obey your betters. Obey, he would.

Still. He would watch her.

"Corley."

"Wok."

"She may resist. Tell her that if she does not come to see me, she will take ill and die."

"Will she?"

"Shek says eat your makeberries every day, does it not?"

"Wok, but—"

"Without them your people cannot survive, whichever world you are in."

Corley tilted his head. "Not-live? I am never knowing this."

"Shek works in mysterious ways. The Murder does not know. Keep it that way."

Keep a secret from his Murder? Not shek-like! But the Morrigan ordered it, and she the top. What could he do?

"Wok," Corley said.

He would keep her secret, and he would do as she asked, for he was Kaa, and Kaa obeyed. He, Corley Drust Fiachra, would fly to the human world and bring his crow-sister back.

CHAPTER SEVEN

Next step: Find a suitable nesting-place.

Well. Before that: Walk. Do not linger because of chickie-lion girls. Do not let your own stumble-bumping stop you. Go.

Without looking back, Fannilea Ishika Fiachra walked, a thing she had never liked to do.

She nestled into the bird fluff coat Leaf had found for her and began, one foot in front of the other. Like a newborn colt unused to its legs, she lurched. Kek, but walking was hard. Crackity-bumps tripped her. And the heaviness! So much of her, there was.

Not like flying, she thought wistfully. But she must forget that, best she could.

She did not know where she was going.

Lost in a world not-yours. Apart from your people, not-right. Nowhere to go, no one to see you. No shek for your living. Lost!

She walked the neighborhood. Big box buildings, small windows, too many people. One dog or two, tethered, but still she eyed them sideways. She ambled, placing her feet with care, watching the houses for the right nest. A half-broken one, like Leaf's, would do.

On a corner some few wing flaps from Leaf's, she found one. She peeked through wood walls closed by a fat lock. Three window levels, not done, but crow-cozy enough. Sign: NO TRESPASSING. She ignored it and slipped between the walls.

No gardens here. Only pebbles. The new nest had no windows or doors, either, but Fannilea didn't mind. She liked the open space, and the long flight and not enough rest had made her sleepy-dim. It was lonely, but it would do.

She crept into the shelter, such as it was, and laid her blanket down. It smelled of lilac, like the chickie-lion girl. In another life, Fannilea would like to know her. Too bad she couldn't now. She placed the bag at one end of the blanket and rumpled it well.

A nest! Not much, but *hers*. Hers alone.

She curled up, well-enough, and sleepy-dim soon turned to not-aware.

The Murder came for her while she slept.

She had known they would come. She had not thought about how.

The middle-day light slanted through the wide-spaces of her new nest and nudged her eyelids open. She yawned and stretched, a fizzy-bright rush of what-to-do filling her head—how much to choose!

Then she noticed the slight figure sitting cross-legged next to her head, waiting and blinking. He made a fair human, with light brown skin and spiky black hair with a white streak on either side—so like his feathers. He wished to be rid of his white, but to Fannilea it showed reckless flair that suited him.

A made-of-yarn poncho hung giant on his thin shoulders—a red, orange, white, black jumbled color-pile. Strings trailed from the armholes. Underneath he wore grungy olive cargo pants and no shoes.

"Did the local crows dress you?" she asked, amused.

"You find me not handsome?" He pouted, with pretend wounds.

Of course the Murder would send her crow-brother. Hadn't they always? But that did not diminish her joy at seeing him. She propelled herself off the floor and fell on him in a tumble of black clothing and white hair and big blue eyes.

"Fannilea Ishika Fiachra," Corley muttered beneath her crushing hug. "It is no good to be going many moons without your self-presence."

"Pfft," she said into his hair. "It has barely been one night, stupid crow."

When they broke apart, Corley pulled his fingers through her hair, gentlelike, running it clean. She made a stop-it face and pushed at him.

"Allopreening is for crows. We are human."

"We are Kaa. And you need it, sister-crow." Corley continued to pet her, oblivious to her frustration.

She peered behind him and all around. "Are there others ... with you?"

"No. No one knows where Corley goes. They would want to share. I get you all, if they don't come. You see?" He grinned crooked, with too much teeth biting one side of his mouth.

She wanted to smile in answerment, but she couldn't. "Oh, Cor," she said. "That's not why. They've sent you to fetch me."

Corley's grin died. "You don't want to come?"

She wobbled. "I have a new nest."

Corley tilted his head, examining the half-built house, cagey-eyed. "This is not a good nest."

"It is *my* nest," she said.

Sharp eyes settled on her face.

"You should come home."

"*This* is my home."

"You are Kaa. The Murder is your home."

"Kek that. I go ahead now, alone."

"You are Kaa, and that is not our way."

"Enough with your pester. I will not go with you. Must we fight?"

His eyes drooped, no longer hot on her face. "No. No pester. No fight."

"Then what have you come for?"

"The Lady speaks of you." Corley's voice-tone held shadow. Shadow often came with mention of the Lady.

The mistress of the Murder. The ruler of the ravens. The goddess of War and Death. The Morrigan.

All who thought upon her trembled with fear.

"What does she say?" Fannilea managed a steady tone, barely.

"She wants to meet with you."

CHAPTER EIGHT

That was it, then. The Murder did not come after all—instead they handed her straight-first to the highest law of the Otherworld, that goddess-witch. Oh the trouble she must be in.

Fannilea tried to calm her breath. She had not expected to escape without notice. She would face up and do what she must; she had resolved on that long ago. But it did not stop her hearts, human and crow, from trembling, though perhaps her crow-heart trembled a shade more.

"I don't want to go back there."

"You must. You know how it is with the Lady."

Ignoring the summons of the Morrigan, for a Kaa, carried a death sentence. The decider of deaths did not like to have her power flouted.

"Besides, the Morrigan says that without makeberries, you will not survive."

"Wok? What nonsense?"

"You will fall ill. Three every day, must have."

As nestlings, they had stayed in the human world to learn of it for weeks at a time. But always there were makeberries, weren't there? Fresh stash in the fridge. Dried in the pockets. Everywhere, always. Shek says, eat your makeberries.

It had not occurred to her that she would *need* them.

She was human! Could she not eat human food? How could she have not known this? Sneaky Murder.

If it were true, she would have to go back. Her hearts hurt. If she were dependent on the berries, how could she ever escape?

"You must fly back with me."

Fannilea sighed. "I am not meant to stay with them. I do not belong there."

"If that is true way down, then they should not be able to keep you. Is that not so?" Corley blink blink blinked, crafty-eyed.

Wasn't it? Shek said the Murder was in her blood, that she would never escape. Hadn't she tried once before and been foiled by her own crow-brother, here now blinking at her?

A nestling of five, she'd been, barely a crow-thing. Newlike. They were living in the human world, training her for the Murder's blood-role, the guidance of the riik, the dead soul's passage, but their time there had ended, and the Murder had to return to the Ahk.

For the first time in a fire-bright way, Fannilea had not wanted this thing. Right in the Murder she had never felt, but this—this burned in her heart, a secret flame not the Murder's. Hers only. She fanned it, and she left them, walking to the safe-making place of the woods. There among the trees, by the trickle-slow water, she had changed.

She had never liked the change. It hurt. It started as a billion tiny pins pinching her skin. Then the pins burst into flame. Blazing fires raged in every joint and ached with the long, slow, hollow pain of age.

Her bones melted, and she screamed.

This was shek.

Her body writhed, and time disappeared. There was only an excruciating burning.

Her eyes watered, and she bit hard on her lip, or—

The white crow hopped down to the bank of the creek, where pools of mud gathered, created by spring snow-melt. The crow waded in to the center of a mud puddle until it was chest-deep and flapped. Mud splattered its feathers, coloring them. The crow thrashed about until not a trace of white showed. Blue eyes peered out of mud-brown feathers. Then the crow hopped up the bank, found the biggest pile of leaves moldering on the woodsy ground, and buried itself.

Time passed. Hard to say how much, for crows and humans see these things differently. Enough to make the muddy nestling stifflike, but not enough for her to feel safe to emerge and move along.

Just as she thought she might not sit still another eye-blink, a crow landed next to the leaf pile. A deep shiny black it was, with white tips on its feathers, but in one more eye-blink it proved to be no crow at all. In its place stood a wiry boy of about six years old with long, glossy dark hair and beady-sharp black eyes.

"Fannilea!" he shouted. "Come out now."

Nothing moved.

"Time to leave!"

No sound was made.

"No choice, not-right," the boy said.

Still no response. He might've been talking to the leaves themselves.

"Pick you up, I will."

This proved too much for the muddy nestling, for she knew that when Corley said these things, he meant them. She would not allow the shame-feel of letting Corley the human scoop up Fannilea the crow.

The pile of leaves exploded. In its midst sat a small human girl with a shock of white hair and big blue eyes peering through the mud on her face.

"You wouldn't," she said, menacing.

"Time to go."

"I'm not." Shoulders square and head high, the girl pushed up and stood ready.

"You are!" the boy shouted.

As nestmates, Fannilea and Corley had tangle-fought often. They dive-bombed, dropped berries on each other, and pulled tails with beaks. They scolded. But it was in fun. They had never—not once—had a real physical fight. She thought he wouldn't hurt her—he was her crow-brother.

But now, there was something needful in his face that she didn't trust.

"Cor?"

"Bring you back, I must."

"Tell them I won't come, and fly away without me."

"Silly! No life without us."

"I will make one. I *like* being human."

"Hush!" Corley fluttered a hand at her face, as to cover her mouth. "Don't say! Against shek, it is."

"I don't care. I don't want to follow shek. I hate it."

"You don't mean that. But do not say it, or erawk-time for you!"

"The erawk isn't real."

"It *is*."

"Then why haven't I seen it?"

"If I were awoah, you would."

Fannilea stuck her tongue out at him.

The Murder whisper-chattered of the erawk, sometimes. None knew if it were real or not. It was not-right to speak of it. It was a place for leaving someone and forgetting them.

"Bring you, I must, Fannilea." Corley spread his legs to stand more stablelike.

"Not-right, you are," she said, and pivoted on her heel and stalked into the woods.

She had barely gone five steps when something barreled into her from behind, knocking her to the ground. She hit hard and lost her breath. She lay on the ground, stunned, struggling to draw air into her lungs. Nothing happened.

Corley pinned her arms behind her back and wrenched one up between her shoulder blades. He sat with one knee digging into the small of her back as the air went out of her.

How she had hated him, then! In the time since, she had come to see that he had only been following his right-life, but … she had thought she would die. She had not given up; she fought hard, but Corley, a year older, had been stronger.

Physically she might still not beat him. But no longer was he stronger where it counted. In the crafty wise ways of the humans … those Murder-crows had magic, but Fannilea had *will*. She would use it.

Corley was right. If she meant to escape, truly, she could do it.

She would meet with the Morrigan, and she would fly back here with a whole pile of makeberries. She would find a way, no matter what the Lady said.

CHAPTER NINE

On the flight back to the Ahk, Fannilea and Corley
played. Nestlinglike, they were. Corley screeched and
dive-bombed, not letting Fannilea drop low. Finally she
had to defend; she fetched an acorn and dropped it on
his head. He yanked her tail. Spiraling, she scolded.

With their games, the long flight passed in an eye-
blink. Before Fannilea had realized they'd crossed the
barrier, the spindly tree of the Ahk came in sight.

The Murder hung about, a horde drenching the branches in black, still and silent, an omen of death.

Fannilea's crow-heart raced, and a flash of fear made her want to turn back.

"Meet with her, you must," Corley said, noticing his crow-sister's discomfort.

"I said I would," Fannilea snapped. Wanting to turn back and actually doing it were not-the-same. But that was Corley. To him desire meant doing.

Hundreds of beady-sharp black eyes followed Fannilea as she and her nestling-mate flew in together. Fearsome though the Murder was, this she could take. Stares meant nothing. Stare back or ignore, she would as she pleased.

It was the beak-opening she feared. That kekking song, rising and burrowing in, and stealing her self-thoughts away. It would come, she knew. Would she be able to resist?

But no Murder beaks opened. No song rose. Her crow-family watched and blinked and remained silent.

Wok? Fannilea looked at Corley. His beak hung open. He had expected to sing.

So Corley hadn't known they wouldn't sing. But if they had sung, he would've turned against her, sung to make her stay. She shouldn't be surprised, for hadn't Corley always obeyed his shek?

Still, he was her crow-brother! Surely that counted for something. He might, at the very least, shut his kekking beak for her.

Especially since none sang a single note. She wondered, but had no time to make answers, for the Morrigan awaited. Fannilea left the silent Murder behind, following the self-same instructions Corley had a short time before.

The stone-place beneath the Otherworld smelt like dead rats. Fannilea wondered if the Morrigan fed them to her ravens or ate them herself. Anything was possible with the goddess, according to the stories.

The damp, dark chamber put her in mind of the erawk. A place for leaving your unwanteds. She thought-stopped those flashes and swooped down to the grotto's perch.

She wished to change; she would have liked to face the goddess as her human-self. But it was not allowed.

The Morrigan-woman sat straight-backed in the spiky-thorned throne.

Fannilea had never seen the Morrigan. Murder-chatter had made her expect a witch, either fierce and frowning or dour and silent, like Death itself.

But the Morrigan was neither. She greeted Fannilea with an upbeat voice-tone, as though she were happy to see her. Her crow-eyes twinkled, and her mouth curled with amusement.

Once, as a nestling in the human world, Fannilea had seen a brother and sister in the park with their mother. The sister sat with a book, reading. But the brother had other ideas—he snuck from behind with a balloon full of water. The Morrigan's face put Fannilea in mind of that boy's tricksy one.

Dour or fierce, she might understand. This, she did not trust. Not one bit.

Silence stretched long between them. Fannilea waited. The Morrigan had called her, after all.

Finally the witch said, "So you have flown off to the human world."

Fannilea waited still.

Delicate as cookie crumbles, the Morrigan said, "You do not wish … to come home?"

"The Ahk is not my home," Fannilea said.

"Without makeberries, you will not survive."

Fannilea still said nothing. Something bigger-dark hid behind the Morrigan's words. The witch would spit it out when she was ready.

"You will need them. You want to take some with you. When you go back."

"Yes."

The Morrigan nodded, sharplike, and Fannilea felt as though she had passed some ancient tryout.

"What if I said that I might be willing to make an agreement with you? An agreement that, if you held your end, would release you from the Murder and all your duties to it?"

Fannilea's beak dropped open; she clacked it shut. No more shek. Could she hope? She must take care, for the Morrigan would not offer this lightlike. Heavy price, it would carry.

"What must I do?" she asked, fear lining her voice-tone with blades.

"I believe there is a half-finished red brick house with a charming rooftop garden somewhere in that city you love so much. I think you know the one. How many people do you suppose live in such a house?"

Fannilea's crow-heart nosedived. Leaf's house. What could the Morrigan want with it?

"Five, do you suppose?" the Morrigan went on. "The leader boy, his sidekick girl, the moonlight girl, her lovesick pup, and the mother-type. Yes, five."

Moonlight girl? Pup? Who were they? And what did the goddess care?

"Five house members. Strangers to you. Humans. The people you wish to live among. What do you think would happen if they knew your true nature?"

"To reveal myself to them would be against shek."

"What care you for shek? Not a fig, I expect. It is what you wish to shrug off, is it not?"

Fannilea had but one answer: "Yes."

"Then I give you this: If you can convince each of the five house members to accept you—to keep you in their fold when they know what you truly are—then I will release you."

"You will not punish me for violating shek?"

"I will not. But if any one of them rejects you, you must return to the Murder and your true home here in the Ahk, without complaint. You must stop rebelling and follow your shek, as it is written for your kind. Understand?"

Fannilea had no idea how she would do such a thing. She didn't know these house members—she barely knew how to be a normal human. But it was her only chance. She knew the Murder too well to think there would be any other.

Without hesitation, she said, "I'll do it."

CHAPTER TEN

The Morrigan tossed her head back, and an ear-hurting laugh like *aw aw aw* echoed in the stone-place. Fannilea hunched, wanting to avoid its ghost-sound.

A tricky smile lingered on the Morrigan's lips. "Oh, child, you are something. Don't you want to think it over? Humans are notoriously changeable. They like you well enough while they think you're one of them, but once they find out you're not …"

Though Fannilea had lived in the human world as a nestling, her contact with humans had been limited. The Murder sheltered its nestlings. They learned only what they needed to lead the riik as an adult, and nothing more. What the Morrigan said could be true.

But it didn't matter. It was her only chance to escape.

"I'll do it," she said again.

"Foolish girl," the Morrigan said. "You haven't even heard the terms."

"Then say them!" Fannilea said, but she knew that the terms would not change her decision.

"You will have two weeks," the Morrigan said.

Fann's beak dropped open. "Two weeks?"

The Morrigan wore a sharp smile, teeth shining.

Fannilea's heart sank. It was insane.

"But—"

"That's nearly three days a person," the Morrigan pointed out. "That seems quite generous to me. Let's see ... two weeks on their calendar brings us to the thirtieth. I'm feeling charitable; I'll give you an extra day. That way you can start your 'new year' right. You know about that, yes? The human celebrations?"

Fannilea hopped in place, without commitment, saying nothing. She did not know the celebrations, and the Morrigan knew it.

The witch cackled again.

"You already agreed, but I'll let you change your mind. We've not signed yet. What do you say, Fannilea Ishika Fiachra?"

Fannilea stepped, one two, turning, until she faced the way she'd come. She wanted to not look at the Morrigan for one thought-moment.

Two weeks—that was no time! Leaf maybe could accept such a thing. But Slate, so full of iron. And the other members? She knew not. But to go back to the Murder … She would not be herself. She would be a shek-bot. Lost, unalive. It was wrong.

She stepped, one two, to face the Morrigan again.

"What is the rest?"

The Morrigan smiled sly. "You're learning, then. One last condition: You will not tell any of the house members of your agreement with me, even after you have told them what you are, until and unless you succeed fully. That is everything."

Fannilea waited, to be sure the witch would add no more. The ravens blinked at her. Finally, she nodded.

"I will do."

The Morrigan reached beneath the throne and pulled out two thick pieces of parchment. She dug into the pile of hair atop her head and found a large raven feather. An inkwell rose from the arm of the throne.

"I like you. Spunky," the Morrigan said as she dipped the feather. "I do believe I'll enjoy breaking you of it if you return." She paused, a glint in her black eye. "*When* you return."

Fannilea ignored her.

"One last chance to back out ..." the Morrigan said, feather hovering.

"I'll sign."

"Good." The Morrigan waved a hand, and one of the ravens advanced on Fannilea.

"Stand still," the Morrigan instructed. "This may hurt a little."

The raven's large, curved beak loomed. It ducked its head and flew toward her. It stretched its neck, curled its head round her neck, and jabbed her, hard.

"Ow," Fannilea cried, more from surprise than pain. A pinch, it was, but she snapped her beak at the raven.

"Here now, quickly," the Morrigan said, pointing at her lap, where the two parchment contracts lay.

Fannilea flew into the Morrigan's lap, and the goddess chivvied her onto the first parchment and motioned tilting her head. Fannilea mimicked the witch, and a thin stream of blood trickled onto the pale paper, staining it an ugly brown.

"Walk through it," the Morrigan instructed, and Fannilea complied, wetting her claws in her own blood and tracking it across the contract, sealing her fate.

The Morrigan replaced the first parchment with the second, and Fannilea repeated her actions.

"Excellent," the Morrigan said, waving her hand once more.

The second raven landed on the witch's shoulder. With a quick burst of motion, he hard-jabbed the Morrigan in the neck as the first raven had Fannilea. A thin rivulet of dark scarlet trickled down her neck. The Morrigan thrust her thumb into the wound, swirling it in blood. Then she brought it down to the page, glistening, and pressed it next to Fannilea's bloody claw prints. When she rolled it away, the contract bore a perfect bloody thumbprint, the Morrigan's seal on Fannilea's destiny.

She followed suit on the second copy.

"Fannilea Ishika Fiachra," she intoned. "You are bound to uphold this contract, as am I, the Morrigan, decider of battles. Keep your side of the bargain and you will be Kaa no longer. Fail, and you shall return and obey. You have agreed?"

"I have," Fann said.

"So mote it be." The goddess rolled both contracts into cylinders and tied each with a piece of twine. She waved her hand one last time, and the first raven snatched up one of the cylinders and took off with it in his beak. In moments he had disappeared into the dark tunnels of the stone-place.

The other copy the Morrigan held out to Fannilea.

Fannilea accepted it, balancing it in her beak.

The Morrigan leaned back. The spiky throne-thorns pricked her shoulders and the nape of her neck, but she did not seem to notice. Blood still trickled down her throat from the wound the raven had made. She did not seem to notice that, either. She bled casually, the scarlet stain like a dark, messy tattoo on her pale skin.

Fannilea's wound had stopped bleeding.

"There is one more thing," the Morrigan said with a settle-right feel.

The second raven flew to Fannilea's perch and landed next to her, something clutched in its beak. It dipped its head, and Fannilea saw—a full pouch. The tangy scent of makeberries rushed her senses, even though its strings were tied.

"Step into the loop."

Fannilea did so, and the raven yanked it tight around her leg.

"Guard them. You will not get more from me."

Fannilea nodded. Flying back would go hard, but at least she was going back.

"You could stay the night, if you liked," the Morrigan said lazily. "If you want one last night in the Ahk. With your people."

Without answering, Fannilea burst into flight.

Below her, the Morrigan cackled.

Fannilea flapped hard, eager to escape the stone-place, eager to escape the Ahk and the Murder and the Morrigan once again. When she emerged into the dead space of the Ahk—the gray light a relief after the dank stone-place—she turned her beak toward the human world and steeled herself for the long journey, weighed down by what she carried, but buoyed by delight—

She had a chance.

She had two weeks.

She had better use them wise.

CHAPTER ELEVEN

We rawk and squawk but in quiet-secret. In whisper-tones, dark and low.

Our white-feathered crow-daughter has made a deal with the Morrigan. The goddess is our right and true leader, and she surely does the proper thing. But … should Murder-orphans be allowed to make deals? How will they learn to obey, as we have?

Some need more teaching than others.

We await the Morrigan. She will explain all. We must have faith, right and true.

Datchett perches above. He gazes upon us fondly. He will take care of us. We need not worry.

Still we flutter and chatter. We do not like topsy-turvy. We prefer everything in its shek-place.

The Morrigan arrives without fanfare. She appears before us in her female aspect in a simple long black gown, her feet bare against the pebbled earth. Black hair and a white stripe cascade over her shoulders, unbound. A circlet of flowers adorns her brow. Her eyes droop, heavy-lidded, veiling her face-look.

"My dear Murder," she begins. "I am sure you've heard that your wayward daughter, the white-feathered crow Fannilea Ishika Fiachra, has come to see me, as I requested. I have bound her to a challenge. She has signed a blood contract, which she cannot escape. Knowing your … proclivities, I expect you would rather I use my power to drag her back immediately. But that would accomplish nothing.

"Datchett and I have discussed Fannilea's long history of … recalcitrance, and it is clear to me that she needs a more serious, lasting lesson. She wants the human world? Let her have it. Let her see what it is all about. Let her experience human relationships. When she sees what they are like, she will come running gratefully back to the Murder, and that will be the end of it. There will be no more escaping. Living with the Murder will seem like a dream when compared with the human world. They are much less forgiving. And so, never fear, my dear Murder, for your white-feathered daughter will be returned to you soon—of her own free will. On my oath as the Morrigan, goddess of War and Death, I promise you that after Fannilea Ishika Fiachra completes her contract, she will not trouble you further."

At this we cheer, loud and faith-full.

CHAPTER TWELVE

One among the Murder did not cheer.

Corley Drust Fiachra did not believe the Morrigan.

He perched apart, not too far (for that was not allowed), but also not as close as he ought. He sat hard, beak drooping, and said not a word to anyone. Slashes of white marred the black of his feathers, dividing his wings like two boldly lit paths through darkness.

How he wished for wings of black like his brethren!

How he longed to believe the way they did, with such a blank purity, untainted.

He listened, not-blinking and feather-still, to the Morrigan. He wanted her words to reassure him—he hoped they would. The goddess strutted, full of confidence, but Corley doubted.

Fannilea would not agree to a challenge she did not think she could win. If she had agreed, then she thought she had a chance. And if she had a chance, and she wanted it enough—and didn't she?—she would find a way.

Fannilea had been a bull-headed nestling, and she had not grown out of it. Corley knew it, even if the Morrigan did not. What would happen if she won?

The Morrigan had signed a blood contract. She would have to honor it. For his crow-sister to sign, the contract must contain the thing she wanted most: to be let loose from the Murder.

Perhaps the Morrigan was willing to risk that, but Corley was not. Perhaps the Morrigan was confident that it would not come to that, but Corley was not. He could not leave it be.

The Morrigan's droopy gaze landed on Corley, and her lips curled up.

Heat stabbed through his crow-breast, and he growled. He tried to thought-stop it; it was against shek, and he wanted to be good, but he hated her.

Something not-right in her, he didn't trust. A stiff cheek-peck, stabbylike, would stop that lip curl. Leave a beak-shaped scar, he would, on that nasty old raven.

These were not good thoughts. He should up-take the Morrigan's truth instead, but when he tried, the heat only burned hotter. He should turn his flaming heart of rage toward faith and do-right, but he could not. He did not trust the witch.

He could not leave it in her hands.

He would have to do something. Something to stop Fannilea winning, something that would ensure her return. Something that would leave no room for doubt.

As the Morrigan dissolved into mist, Corley Drust Fiachra was not reassured one bit. He resolved to take matters into his own wings.

To bring his crow-sister back, he would do whatever he had to.

CHAPTER THIRTEEN

Fannilea rang the doorbell of the boarded-up red brick house with the rooftop garden at approximately nine o'clock of the human hour that night. Despite her burdens, and despite fierce weather, she had flown back from the Ahk in record time.

As she had crossed into the human world, the wide-open sky poured down upon her, soaking her feathers in an eye-blink. The wind had blown water drops sideways; they stung her eyes, so she closed them and flew blind. She had struggled on, undaunted—she had left the Murder. She would fly in rain and wind to a place where she had no home over and over if it meant no more shek.

Back at her makeshift nest, she changed to human and dressed herself in the clothes Leaf had given her. She had no towel for hair-drying, but it mattered not, for she went straight back out in the rain.

Now she stood on the stoop, with drip-drop hair and heavy clothes, wet in her bones, hoping Leaf would answer her ring and not a stranger.

A great ugly fright-ache gripped her belly. Some of her sparkle-joy had worn off; here she faced what next. She didn't like it; she didn't want to ask these people for anything. What was she to say?

Please, I need your help. Kekking ugly, it was. What reason did they have to help her? None.

To escape the Murder, she had to get into the house. She had to make them like her. She had no idea how to do that. She didn't think even the Murder liked her. If they did, it was only shek. Even Corley? Maybe.

The door opened, and Slate peered into the driving rain. Fannilea could not stop the buzz of fire in her heart at the sight of that hard-lined mouth once more. But when the iron-eyed boy saw her, his brow creased and his face darkened.

"Leaf!" he yelled. "Your *caso triste* is back!"

Fannilea didn't want to ask him to be let in. She hugged herself, water dripping into her eyes—she couldn't tell if it was from her soaked hair or new rain. Words did not come out. She couldn't make them.

Slate wandered away. He left the door open, but he had not invited her in. She stayed where she was.

Leaf appeared, hurrying down the stairs and into the front hallway. "You left her out in the rain?" she yelled.

She wide-smiled at Fann, so true and not-hiding. "Come to pay me back already?"

"No," Fannilea whispered. "I can't." I need more help, she wanted to say, but could not. So she said the only other thing she could think of: "I want to help with the garden."

Leaf opened the door farther. "Get in here, you strange bird," she said.

Fannilea stepped into the front hallway. It hugged her with steam-warm air and soft gold light. Leaf disappeared and returned with a giant fluffy towel, which she threw over Fann's hair, covering her eyes. Fannilea froze, captured. Hands gripped her head and tumbled her hair, tangle-jangling and squeeze-stripping until it dripped no more.

"There!" Leaf said, pulling the towel back so Fann could see. "Better? You'd better get changed, too. Borrow my flannel jammies if you want."

"I ... why are you so doing-things? For me?" Fannilea blurted.

Leaf shrugged. "I like you. You're interesting."

"You don't know."

"I know enough," Leaf said. "Would you like it better if I were mean, like Slate?" A sly smile played at her lips.

Fannilea squeezed her laughter back—she didn't want to sound of crow with Leaf so nice. It might stumble-block this good moment.

"Go and change, and then we'll talk about the house, OK? You do want to stay?"

Fannilea nodded, claws in her throat.

Upstairs, she took the pajamas from Leaf's nest pile into the room next door, the one Leaf said could be hers. Hanging from an old nail in the wall was the white-feathered mask that had been on the bench when she'd flown in. Had Leaf known she would come back?

She stripped off her wet clothes in a think-fog. Leaf's flannel pajamas smelled of lilac, like the chickie-lion girl herself. Fannilea stuffed her face in them and breathed in. So comforting, it was.

Maybe staying here would be all right. Maybe it was not like the Murder.

Maybe she could win this contract.

The skin-feel of the lilac-smelling bedclothes brought a rosy-warm niceness into her belly. It was a small thing, pajama loan—to Leaf. But to Fann … the only thing she had, in this eye-blink.

She did not like to let it be unreturned. She wanted to do something.

But what could she offer Leaf? She had nothing.

No, not true. She had hands. Mind. Body, even if not strong. Work, she could work. But work they all must.

What else? What she alone might have …

Fannilea bounded down the stairs, flush with plans.

"I will return your niceness," she crowed.

"You don't have to," Leaf said. "It's not—"

"Yes. I do. Tomorrow, I will meal-find, and I will bring you eats. Delicious eats."

"Meal-find?"

"Oh—another word. There must be."

Leaf winced. "Dumpster dive?"

"That doesn't sound nice," Fann said, frowning.

Leaf grinned. "It's not. It's nice of you to offer, but we tried a while back and didn't find much."

"I have special ways."

Leaf chewed a fingernail, studying Fann. "Yeah? Well, I don't mind trying again. Maybe I'll come, too."

"No, you stay. My giving. For pajama-borrowing. And clothes. All the niceness."

"Seriously, I didn't need those clothes. You're a strange girl, Fann, but you're all right. I have a feeling you're just weird enough to belong here …"

Kek, Fannilea thought, I hope chickie-lion girl is right. With both hearts alike.

CHAPTER FOURTEEN

The next morning, Fannilea Ishika Fiachra called upon the crows.

Standing on the rooftop of the red brick house, she planted her feet and threw her head back. Then she opened her human-beak and sang out the Kaa call for a fledgling seeking eats-help.

The locals would have their own version, but they would recognize the Kaa. The ferriers of the dead and the crow-birds of the living world had a bond—to help the Kaa survive in the human world, the crows shared. An extension of the Murder, it was. Or so they told her.

As a nestling, Fannilea had questioned Manak about it. "Do they want to help us?"

"There is no want. They are crows."

"Like shek?"

"Yes. Like shek."

For Fannilea, the question-feel lingered. Did the bond vex them? Something about the way they turned shifty-footed whenever the Murder called made her uncomfortable. She didn't like it much.

Still, they helped when called, and she must ask them to help her now, for she had nothing else to offer the house of humans.

The crows appeared, one by one. Their dark bodies peppered the power line. Before long, they buried it, the ledge of the house, and every other perchable surface in sight. They shuffled claws and fluffed feathers. Here in front of them, a crow-girl without her Murder. Did it discomfit them? But it was no matter, they could not break the long-had bond.

The crows showed her three good meal-find spots, and Fannilea tried to give as much thanks as she could, though she saw that it didn't comfort them. When they had fulfilled their duty, the crows departed in a dark cloud of wings.

Satisfied, Fannilea hopped downstairs. On the stairwell, she met Leaf, wearing torn-up clothes and carrying the feather jacket she had given Fann.

Leaf pinchy-peered at her, curiouslike, but all she did was shrug and say, "I brought your coat."

Fann stuffed her arms into the puffy coat.

In this way, together the helpful chickie-lion girl in black and the white-feathered girl who talked to crows set out into the streets of Brooklyn to meal-hunt. Fannilea led the way, using the sense-directions the crows had given, and Leaf followed.

A couple of blocks away loomed Food Bazaar, the largest grocery in the neighborhood. The two girls followed the building's walls around to the back. Several large dumpsters pressed against the back wall; Fannilea pushed back a squawk, but part of it escaped. She pointed to distract Leaf—"Look!"

On top of the dumpster sat a clean cardboard box. Fannilea pushed the flaps open. Leaf stood on tiptoe to see over her shoulder. Inside, they found plastic-wrapped sandwiches, single-serving salads, cold cuts, a cheese tray, a vegetable tray, and a six-pack of single-serving chocolate milk.

"Weird," Leaf said.

Fannilea started loading the food into a bag.

"Store people leave it for ones without," she said. The crows had told her that even some regular people foraged in this town—such a place!

"Sure, but how did you know it would be here? Have you been to this store before?"

Fannilea shook her head.

"Do you know the owner or something?"

"A great idea, that is. Meet owners! Make friends."

Leaf chewed her lip but didn't comment.

They left the grocery, and Fannilea turned the corner as the crows had instructed. At the end of the block, a restaurant occupied the corner. All Fannilea and Leaf had to do this time was follow the food-scents. French fry-smell wafted down the alley to the street corner.

Here they had to climb into the dumpster, but inside they found two big paper bags of french fries, a huge bag of fried chicken, and two boxes of assorted fresh fruit and vegetables. Unable to resist, Fannilea stuffed four french fries in her mouth.

"Yum," she said, after she'd swallowed. "Want some?" She offered one of the bags to Leaf.

"No," Leaf said, laughing. "Too early."

"Never too early for french fries," Fann said, having another four.

The two girls filled their totes, climbed out of the dumpster, and started walking back to the red brick house. It was a good stash, they had.

"One more stop," Fannilea said. "Up there." She waved vaguely at the street they were on. The crows had not been too specific about this stop, and she hadn't quite been able to understand what they meant to point her toward. Food-help but not food. Or something like that.

"These are all houses," Leaf said. "I don't think there will be food here. And it's not trash day. What do you think we're going to—oh, what's that?"

About two hundred yards ahead of them on the sidewalk was a small Weber grill with a handwritten sign on it that said FREE, PLEASE TAKE.

"Ohhh . . ." Leaf said. Her face slackened with a deep-seated want. "We've wanted a grill for the house for so long! It's small, but it'll work."

Skittering forward, Leaf scooped up the little black grill and cradled it in her arms.

"This is going to be the most amazing Sunday dinner ever!" she said happily. "We'll introduce you to everyone and propose your membership. We offer a two-week trial membership to new members."

Fann frowned. "This is a big deal?"

"Don't worry," Leaf said. "Everyone's going to love you. I mean, you do want to share this food, right? You don't have to, of course; it's yours. I just thought—"

"I could stay? And not share?"

"Of course."

Fannilea grimaced. "But the house members will like it? If I do share?"

Leaf nodded. "This is an amazing spread."

"Then I will share."

Something not-right squeezed Fannilea's chest. Was she doing something wrong? She couldn't tell. Wasn't this good? It would help the house members like her, right? Her contract depended on that. So it must be good. Why did it feel not-right?

As they neared the house, Leaf stopped short.

"No," she muttered. "Not again."

"What? What is it?" Fann peered around her.

On the sidewalk ahead, in front of the house, sat a large black crow, picking at a fat french fry.

"It's a crow," Leaf said, skirting the bird and turning toward the house.

"W—er—yes?" Fannilea said. "That's a problem?" She clicked her teeth at the thing, hoping it would fly off, but it only stopped eating and stared at her. She bared her teeth at it; it didn't flinch.

"Yes," Leaf said, a heavy weight in her voice. "Slate hates them."

Fannilea deep breathed, slow and long, trying not to burst. *Of course* Slate kekking hated crows. Because why should it be easy?

"Why?" She fought to keep a steady voice-tone.

"I don't know. No one in the house knows. He won't talk about it." Leaf shook her head. "It's weird that it's here. When they finally went, I didn't think they would ever come back."

"When they went?"

"Slate got rid of them."

Fannilea bit her thumbnail. Crows weren't easy to get rid of. She feared the answer but asked the question anyway.

"How?"

"Oh, he tried everything. Fake predators, loud noises. Nothing worked. But apparently crows have a thing about not wanting to be somewhere where a crow has been killed. So he caught one, wrung its neck, and hung its body up in the backyard. It sounds gruesome, I know, but it worked."

So Slate, her new housemate, on whom her future freedom depended, in part, and who she also had some kind of unknown electric feel for ... was a crow-killer.

Kekking fantastic.

CHAPTER FIFTEEN

"Everything's ready," Leaf said, appearing in the doorway of Fannilea's bedroom.

"Everyone keeps asking where the food came from. I think Slate suspects, but I made him keep quiet. C'mon! I'm so excited!"

Fannilea dragged her feet. Strange, these humans were. She still couldn't tell if they had Murders of their own, or if this was one. She hadn't thought, but … it felt like part of one, this thing Leaf expected. Like ritual. It made Fannilea uneasylike.

Leaf had decided that Fannilea should hide until dinner—to surprise the other house members. Fannilea had gone along, letting Leaf know best. Now, facing three new-meets, she wished she'd said no. But she had no choice except to hop downstairs behind Leaf and into the glowing kitchen, where dinner (and the new-meets) waited.

"Ta-da!" Leaf thrust her arms toward Fann. "Everyone! This is Fann. She's responsible for the ridiculous feast you're about to eat," Leaf said.

A girl reached for a top cupboard, her back to Fannilea. Tree girl, Fann thought, for she had shining skin of wood color and ever-long limb-branches. She wore dark jeans and a collar shirt, extra crispy. Wool-curly hair for leaves and strong no-shoes feet for roots.

"This is Jayda," Leaf said, "the only one in the house who uses her real name."

Fannilea huddled there in the doorway, birdlike, uncertain, feeling not-human.

With a stack of colored plates, the girl spun round.

Her brown ember-gaze met Fann's, and she danced across the kitchen, bringing an orange scent, warm energy, and a join-us smile.

Fannilea wanted to trust, but how?

Jayda circled behind her. Breath-whispers ruffled Fannilea's neck hairs. Was the girl herding her?

"Come, meet the others," Jayda said. Her shoulder bumped Fannilea's, and the tree-girl chivvied the crow-girl through the kitchen.

Fannilea's food pile covered the table. On the other side, Slate pressed against the wall, eyeballing the food. Fannilea couldn't tell what that look meant. He dealt her a glance like a blow, then went back to the food. He did not look hungry.

Two more new-meets stood by the table, a girl and a boy. The boy brushed food crumbs from his mouth with shrugged shoulders. Fann met his sorry look with a secret smile, for she saw which plate he'd grabbed from—french fries.

"This is Moonbeam," Leaf said, pointing to the girl.

Moonbeam surely had her name from that long, straight, moonlit hair. Made of reeds, she was, like the branch of a willow. Shiny silver circles dazzled at her ears and her fingers.

"Grilling in December," she said, her words honey-slow. "You must think we're crazy."

"We are," said the boy. Twig-colored hair dusted caterpillar eyebrows behind big round wire rims. Confused and younglike, he seemed, but wide, smartish blue eyes showed it not true.

"This is Scrap," Moonbeam said, one arm lifting. "Watch out. He'll try to make you shake his *left* hand, cause he's a lefty and uppity about it. He's tolerable because he doesn't talk much, though."

"Moonbeam would like for me to not talk much," Scrap said. "Whether I do or not is a matter of some debate. In sum, don't listen to anything she says, especially about me. She's incredibly biased."

"In your favor," Moonbeam shot back.

"S'what I meant." Scrap winked.

Fannilea teetered, unbalanced.

"Are you taking the room next to Leaf's, then?"

"Oh, you should!" Moonbeam's eyes glowed. "We have plenty of room."

Fannilea's crow-heart trembled. Had she been wrong to think she could live here like this? It was too much.

"You *are* going to stay, aren't you?"

She had lost her tongue.

But iron-boy had found his. He pushed off, slowlike, and stood straight with stone shoulders.

"So, you brought the food," he said slowly, surveying the table. "Where'd you get it?"

"That's the thing," Leaf said excitedly. "We meal-found—I mean, we dumpster dove! But she knew exactly where to find good stuff. It wasn't like when we went before."

"How did you know where to go?" Slate's winter-cold eyes pecked at her.

Somehow Fannilea did not think that iron-boy would be so easy about ignoring her odd-self, like Leaf. "Special ways" would not be enough.

"I have friends," she tried. "They know good spots."

"If you have friends here, why aren't you staying with them?"

"They … are not that kind of friends."

"Leave her be! What's your problem?"

Slate's expression didn't change.

Leaf barreled on. "I ... I wanted to propose that we start her on a two-week trial. With the aim of making her a member."

Several things happened at once.

Fannilea cringed.

Moonbeam said, "Cool ..."

Tree-girl Jayda leapt up from the table, yanked a paper from the fridge-front, and stuffed it at Fannilea.

After that, sounds blurred. Time slowed. Underwater, Fannilea was. The people cawed at her, but they sounded hollowlike and far-off. She rubbed her ears to check for pinfeather stuffing.

The paper in her hands read HOUSE CHARTER in tall letters at the top. Someone had plunked "Shady" before "house" in tiny crow-scratch letters.

It was a list of must-dos.

... THREE HOURS WORK A WEEK ...

... KNOCK ON DOORS ...

.... DISCUSS ISSUES ...

Leaf's voice rang out. "It doesn't even say you have to come to Sunday dinner."

"But you do," Scrap said in a low-growl voice.

It was a play voice, like her crow-brother Corley sometimes used, but just then it didn't sit right with Fannilea. She couldn't focus. The thing that kept drawing her eye-gaze was that scribbled-in word.

"Shady …?" she asked, faintlike.

"Shady House!" Scrap said gleefully. Then he burst into song.

The tune, had she heard it before?—but the words, something not-right about them—

Here's a story of a house named Shady
Which was full of three very lovely girls
One of them had hair of silver, like on the bottle
The others had darker curls

The others joined. Moonbeam sang way-big, while Jayda bell-tinkled. Leaf laughed too much.

Only Slate did not open his human-beak.

Here's a story of a house named Shady
Which was also home to two handy boys

They were five kids living all together
Yet they were all alone

Til this one day when the girls and boys of Shady
Guessed that they were in some sort of crunch
That this group must somehow form a family
That's the way they all became the Shady Bunch

But Fannilea stopped hearing that song. Instead she heard a crow-song, the one she'd heard since nestlinghood, again and again and again. A song that squeezed her breath out, so tight it had followed her here, from that other world.

The house members sang the Het Ket Wok Aw Aw.

It could not be so, she knew, yet she heard it.

"Sing with us, Fann!" they urged.

"Yes, sing with us!"

She ought to. It would be uncountable time in the erawk for her if she didn't. Datchett grew more hard-beaked. His shek-force didn't work on her. She came out with more iron in her heart. More alone rather than together. But she didn't want to go back to the erawk.

Fannilea trembled. Oh goddess they were a Murder. She had escaped one only to be bound to another. What had the Morrigan gotten her into?

CHAPTER SIXTEEN

A voice of steel halted the song.

"No," it said.

Danger-voice, that boy had. A stopping of all. His eyes held iron again. But ... was there something else? Something underneath? Hurtlike. But how could she see this in only an eye-blink of knowing him? It was impossible. She was thought-wishing.

"No singing. You're not staying."

"Fann, could you give us a moment?" Leaf glared at Slate. "We, the house members, have something we need to discuss."

"Please. Stay I would like." Fannilea fumbled her words. Urgent need buzzed in her bones. They could not shut her out now. "Say all words before me, even about my own-self; I like better to know it. Don't fear talking."

"It would be better if—"

One look made Leaf sigh. Already she understood Fann's yes-you-will.

"Fine. I want to go ahead and put it to a vote. Fann gets a two-week trial and a chance at membership in the house. I vote yes."

"It doesn't matter," Slate said.

Leaf ignored him. "Who else is in favor?"

Sideways-eyeballing Slate, Moonbeam raised her hand, slowlike. "Look at this food, *meng*," she said. "It's unbelievable."

"I like her," Jayda said, firm, also raising her hand.

"You guys know I do whatever Moonbeam tells me to do," Scrap said.

Fannilea couldn't tell if he was serious or not. But he raised his hand. Four raised hands. They all wanted her to stay. Except Slate. Her crow-heart beat hard. Would Slate agree?

"You remember that I have final word over new house members?" Slate sounded down-low. He watched the floor, not them.

Leaf made hard fists and jaw. "That's because I trusted you to use it responsibly. Not from caprice."

"It's not caprice. You don't know."

"Then let her stay."

"I can't. She can't."

"Why not?"

Slate had turned his back. He faced the picture window and the patio door, which looked out onto a small backyard. Had he seen the same crow Fannilea and Leaf had seen on the sidewalk earlier? Could that be what this was about?

"It doesn't matter," he said. "I'm using my veto. I'm head of the house, and I don't want her here."

Fannilea needed in so she could win her contract, not a question. Without the house, she would be lost. And yet … this say-so of the iron-boy's made her feel something right. She breathed. The thought of no must-do lifted her insides like flying.

She did not like that kekking contract. Ugly feel, it had, even if it was going to get her free of the Murder.

"Not even a trial membership? What is going on?"

"The house charter states that I have final word over all new house members. It doesn't say I have to explain my decisions."

"Maybe not," Leaf said, with creasy-brow and angry eyes. "But our friendship does. I like this girl, I think she'd be good for the house, and I want her to stay. If you have a problem with her, then explain."

"I can't."

"Then I don't know if I can stay here myself."

"You'd break up the house over her? And break up our friendship?"

Fannilea cringed. She didn't want that, either.

"Not over her. I thought we had a friendship based on openness. I thought *the house* was based on that. But this …" Leaf shook her head, eyes closed.

Slate pivoted. He gaze-met the house members.

"You'll say I'm crazy," he said.

A fear-shiver bolted down Fannilea's spine.

"Try me," Leaf said. "Have I ever?"

They kept eye to eye for a long time, with no words. When the eye-blinks had stretched, he said, "I never told you this."

He waved for them to come to the window. Fann stayed feather-still, not wanting to intrude, as the others crossed.

"*Mira*," Slate said, and pointed out the window.

At the far back of the yard grew a giant pine tree. Fannilea saw at once why Slate was alarmed. Feathered black menace-spots covered every inch of tree, huddled with beaks tucked away for the night.

Crows.

Come to roost at Shady House.

On the same day as Fannilea Ishika Fiachra had.

"The crows are back," Leaf said. "I know. We saw one on the sidewalk this morning."

No one else said a word.

After a long white silence, Leaf whisper-wondered, "You think the crows came back because of Fann?"

"One year of not a single crow near the house, and then the *day* she returns and wants a trial membership, an *entire roost* lands in our backyard."

Hurt-feel and not-understanding mixed on Leaf's face. "They're *crows*, Slate. Birds."

"I told you," Slate said. "You won't understand."

"Explain it to me. Please."

Yes, Fannilea thought—explain. Where did that fear-feel come from? So deep. So long. Humans and animals did not like this kind of fight. Not usual. Not with regular crows.

Did Slate know something he shouldn't?

"It's strange."

"It's strange? You have no particular reason for connecting the two, and you have no other reason for not wanting Fann in the house. Just, it's strange."

"Yes. You need to trust me. That *is* why you told me I should be head of the house and have the veto, right? Because you trust me? I can't say more. That's it."

Watching the not-moving stone-shape of Slate's shoulders, Fannilea did not think this was true.

Neither did Leaf.

"You know, I did trust you. I thought I could. But I also thought you would *talk to me*. I see I was wrong." Leaf turned to the other house members. "Fann and I will start looking for a new place to live first thing in the morning. If any of you would like to join us, please let me know." Knife edges bled into her tone. "But please, no crow haters. Just in case Slate's right, and an entire roost of crows follows Fann wherever she goes."

She stalked out of the room.

Slate stood brittle, a hand on the doorknob as if he were about to fly off, too. The stone had not left his shoulders nor the iron his eyes. Stifflike, he turned, and his metal gaze fell on Fannilea.

Anger, there was not. His eyes cloud-fogged now, looking far-off, not at her. A longtime feeling of not-right, she could see. Her hearts broke, human and crow, for she did not like to bring trouble.

She would fix it, she resolved. Both this breach between friendy and friendy and the clouds in that boy's eyes. She would think of something.

Still she wondered, what secret was he hiding?

CHAPTER SEVENTEEN

In the dead of the dark December night, moonless, the backyard of the red brick house lay still. The crow roost slept on, not-minding the snap-tight quiet of the human household.

Slate said that Fannilea could stay the night, if she left at day-rising. Leaf wanted to sleep-think, but told Fannilea she thought she would go with her.

Fann had a better idea.

When the house fell quietlike, she crept downstairs. She had seen a door, near the kitchen. Leaf had said the basement was for storage. It would be the place, she thought, to find the needful thing. It scared her, but she could not let Leaf leave the house.

Taking a deep breath, Fannilea twisted the knob and swung the door open. A wooden stairwell descended into empty black.

So like the erawk.

What if the humans meant to lock her down there? What if they were planning to throw her in it? What if the Morrigan had known, had handed her off to another kind of Murder . . .

No, she must stop. No one knew she was down here. It was a storing-place. For things. Not people. This was not the Murder. This was not the erawk.

Her heart still wild-thumped.

She had to go down. But she could decide how.

Leaving the door open, she crossed back through the kitchen, eased open the last drawer on the end, and peeked at the bits and bobs inside, hoping her thought-guess was right.

Finally, feeling around at the back, she found what she needed—a point-light. She pressed the button and a dim light beam pooled on the tile.

Satisfied, Fannilea returned to the door. Tongue-biting to help her fear less, she shined the light on the stairs and started down.

A barely-there railing hung half-on, half-off the wall. Fannilea didn't touch it. She hopped down the steps, one at a time.

Halfway down, she stopped. Something had caught the edge of the light beam. There, at the stair bottom, silver gleamed. Fannilea whuffed with triumph.

Keeping the light on the metal, she hop-stepped the rest of the way down the stairs. There, the silver gleam resolved into a rectangular metal box made of spider web–thin steel wires. It had two doors, one on each side. Put a tempting-tasty pile of peanuts inside, and when a bird hopped along to have breakfast, snap! Caught, he was.

An erawk for regular crows.

Her poor bound brethren. But Slate had to let her into the house, and she could think of no other way.

While the others slept, she had cut holes in a cloth strip. Now she pulled it out and tied it over her face. Crows memory-marked predators, and she could not let them do it to her. She would need them still. She didn't like it, but she would have to fool them.

All because of that kekking contract. It was to be her salvation, but … she did not like the way of it.

She lugged the trap up the stairs. Clutching it close, she quiet-stepped across the room and eased the patio door open.

The roost didn't stir. Fannilea crept into the yard.

Chairs littered the lawn, some plastic, some metal, one wood. A wrought-iron bench, twin to the one on the roof, faced into the yard.

She padded through the grass and around the tree, as far as she could get from the house. Farther from humans, she would like, but this would have to do.

She laid the trap near the fence, in the shadow of the pine. From her Leaf-shirt pocket, she pulled a jar of peanuts she'd lifted from the kitchen. Shaking a pile of them into her hand, she crouched. Delicatelike, she placed peanuts in a line into the trap.

A sharp voice out of the dark made her flinch.

"What are you doing?"

As she peered toward the door, a lanky frame with spiky hair took shape. Iron-boy eyeballed the box.

"You scared me," she said, not-stopping. She placed more peanuts.

"That's mine."

"I found it in the basement."

"Stole it, you mean."

"I didn't steal it, you—" Swear, she wanted to, but stopped. "I'm setting it up. In *your* backyard. It'd be better with dog food"—Fannilea wrinkled her nose; she hated dog food, but most crows gobble-gulped it down—"but peanuts will work."

"You're trying to catch a crow."

"Astonishing, your figuring-out abilities, they are," she said. More peanuts placed. "Crows," she added, "are not easy to shake. Kekking pests."

A hint of a smile lit Slate's eyes, pale behind the thunderclouds but clearly there. Small it was, but still enough to send a burst of hope through Fannilea's human-heart. She sat on her knees and tilted her head up, wanting a better look. Contained, he was, in himself. Alone, apart, wrong. Like her. Not like Kaa who were all together. Part of each and everyone and everything. For true, he was lovely. An earth-moving feel shook her. She dropped her eyes and focused hard on peanut-laying.

"You're doing that because of what I said, that you couldn't stay," he said, watching.

"If I make the crows go, you would not mind."

"You want to stay so much?"

"It is the *most* important thing."

She opened one door of the cage and laid the last of the peanuts inside. Then she set the spring. "I know about crows. I know how they chase. You are not wrong to want them away."

"They showed up when you did. One is connected to the other."

Fannilea considered. She did not want to tell the not-truth. But she could not yet tell it true, either.

"I won't say that it isn't. Everywhere I go, there are crows. But that doesn't mean I want them there."

Slate frowned, never taking his gaze from her face.

Fann wondered. What could he tell, from her eyes? If she might betray him? So aware in his looking, he was, she thought he might tell exactly that. Not like the Kaa, only sharp-eyed for what they were supposed to see. Staring right at the true thing, not knowing. Not this one. Find the truth, he would, whether supposed to or not. Find it first, and then decide what it meant.

A violent want hit her—for him to say she could stay.

Not because of the contract. Not because of the others. Not because of any thing but one: She wanted him to want her there.

But she would not beg. She only looked back, and let him see what he could in the blue-shining of her human eyes.

They both kept still.

After a long-passing, he said, "Okay. For now. You can have the trial."

"Whoop whoop," Fann whispered, a smile breaking.

His iron look had sunshine behind it. "You have to understand how the house works. There aren't a lot of rules, just enough to live together in peace, but the ones we have are serious."

"OK," she said.

She was in. One step closer. It didn't matter what she had to do; she would. Except ... "Do I have to sing that song?"

His laugh fell like a broad stroke of sound. Fann wanted to move inside of it.

"That ridiculous thing! ... No. But ... there is one thing you should know. None of us are of age to live here on our own legally, so we can't have anyone poking around. I don't know your story, but keep yourself together. If you go to school, or to work, or wherever, be normal. Everything's fine, when you're out there. Need to lose it, go crazy, be a weirdo, you do it here. Understand?"

Fannilea knew about keeping her right face on. That, she could do.

But ... the other bit ... if you needed to lose it, it was okay? If she did not keep her right face on, here, with the house-humans, what would happen? Nothing? She would be okay, they would be okay? No erawk. No words of punishment. No shunnings.

Was that what a real home was like?

CHAPTER EIGHTEEN

And so Fannilea Ishika Fiachra, crow-girl and Kaa guide of the Ahk, Otherworld, became a trial member of Shady House of Bushwick, Brooklyn, New York, USA, human world.

Stay for two weeks, she would, as a maybe-member of the house, and then the others would decide if she could stay for good.

The last day of her trial would also be the last day of

her contract with the Morrigan. If all went as it ought, Fannilea would be deciding her own fate that day.

But she thought-stopped that. For now, she had one goal: become part of the house.

Strange it was, for her.

Fannilea had never had a true home. The mother who laid her egg and the father who seeded it had not wanted her. She did not even know who they were.

Among her people, she was a white-feathered thing in a sea of black—an ill omen.

If the Murder had had its way, she would have been left for dead. She nearly was, but for one who refused to let her suffer that fate. She did not know how he'd been allowed, but Manak Deshai Fiachra had claimed her as his own daughter and raised her alongside his son, Corley Drust.

In this way, Fannilea had gained a family of sorts. But she had never forgotten that her born-parents did not want her. She could not forget it.

She knew that Manak must know who they were— everyone in the Murder knew all of everyone else, and if they did not, then they either found it out or made it up and spread it around as truth—but she never asked. She did not want to know.

Shady House had much more home in it than the Ahk. Color in all places. Food, such food! Her space apart. Bliss, it could be. But if she wanted it to last, she could not rest. She must do.

She brought gifts. Crowish, but it was something.

For the moonlit girl, snack-sized bags of Cheetos, though the thought of eating those orange powdered wood-bits gave Fannilea nose wrinkles. Like crows with dog food, something not-right about that. She also brought patchouli oil, which she bought with the money she earned from the house members in exchange for meal-finding.

For the tree girl, papaya. She liked to eat it at breakfast, and it was sometimes hard to get. Also tinkly silver wrist-bangles, for their prettiness and so Fann would have a warning when she walked up behind.

For Scrap, sunflower seeds and lemon-lime soda. She found also a poster of a man with fly eyes, in a suit of red and blue with black web-bits everywhere. She had seen Scrap with a magazine-book about this man.

For Leaf, a garden-trellis. A big, black silk flower. Dark chocolate with mint.

Tougher, Slate was. She hard-thought for many times but couldn't know. She brought him a cheeseburger with fries. He said "thank you" like he didn't know what cheeseburgers were for.

They asked her what they could give her in return.

"Nothing," she said, with a shame-flash.

It was supposed to be true, but it wasn't. But she wanted their acceptance, and she did not like saying "nothing," not one kekking bit. It reminded her of the Murder. They said "nothing" like that a lot. But there was always something. Always, always something.

The house members said she didn't have to give them things. But when she insisted, they accepted.

It wasn't enough. No matter how right, gifts were impersonal. The crow way.

Fannilea wanted to do things that would *matter*.

Moonbeam worked part-time as a barista at a coffee shop, but she had trouble getting up for work, even when her shift was in the afternoon. She was not a morning person. Fann could help with that.

The girl posted her work schedule on the fridge. Fannilea checked it close Wednesday night; Moonbeam was supposed to work at 10 a.m. on Thursday.

At 9 a.m., Fann eased into Moonbeam's bedroom, closed the door behind her, and crossed to the hammock Moonbeam slept in. Then she opened her human-beak and warbled a made-up tune at the top of her not-good singing voice.

Moonbeam woke growling and shooed Fann from the room as though she were a true crow. Why was beyond Fannilea's ken.

Jayda, who took a special college fashion class through her school, had a big essay due at the end of the week. Fannilea worked through the night, writing and writing and writing. Not perfect, her words, but it would be a place to start and the tree girl might fix them. She left the pages on Jayda's desk at day-rising.

But Jayda did not seem pleased.

"Fann? Is this your handwriting?" Like she had done something wrong.

Fann nodded.

"This is my fashion homework."

"Had to be done?" She wanted to help—how could that be wrong?

"Yes. By me. I—this is what I want to do with my life, Fann. I have to learn it. I get that you wanted to help, but ... don't touch my stuff without my permission."

Two of these strange reactions would not deter Fannilea. She would do the next one right. Find the right thing. There must be something.

On Friday night, Fann and Scrap had dinner together; the others were out. Fann shared her meal-found sandwich, and Scrap made frozen waffles with blueberry jam and peanut butter.

As they ate, he confessed that he and Moonbeam were a band.

"Well, not a band, exactly," he said. "But we make music. She doesn't like anyone to know. Sometimes we sit out in the backyard and sing, when I can talk her into it. Do you want to see my guitar?"

There were many half-broken, beat-up things at Shady House, but Scrap's guitar was the hardest-beaten. Scratched-rough and dinged-up, it had a word carved into its body—WHEN. Strings had broken and curled. What kind of music could it make?

"I keep meaning to restring," he said with a sorry-sound. "I haven't gotten around to it."

"I can do it," Fann said. "To help."

Scrap wrapped his arm around the side of the guitar and pulled it closer to his stomach.

"You don't have to. I'll do it."

"I want to help."

"I … that's nice. But I want to do it myself."

Fann frowned. "Myself! Myself! That's what everyone says."

"Well … don't you have anything like that? Something that belongs to you, that you don't want other people to touch?"

Fannilea didn't know what to say. The only thing she wanted was to be free of the Murder. Until then, nothing else was any use.

But that was what she was doing, wasn't it? It was her thing that belonged to her. And she got closer to it by helping them, didn't she? But she couldn't tell him that, by dint of her contract.

So she did not help Scrap, which made her feel not-right. She thought that this might make him not like her, but something about that made her feel not-right, too. She didn't know what.

But still there were Leaf and Slate, and just because the other three did not want her help did not mean these two would not. She couldn't give up.

So she turned her attention to the rooftop garden. She had brought a trellis home for Leaf and showed her, but they had done nothing with it yet. Leaf drew her a picture of it set up over the bench with ivy-sprangles and lanterns hanging.

Fannilea set to work. She made the vision, in the night, bit by bit. When the lights were hung, she plug-started them, and the rooftop glowed, a new heaven place. Leaf would love it.

In the morning, Fann made the chickie-lion girl put on a cloth-mask. She led her up to the roof to show what she had made. She told Leaf to sit on the bench, and then she removed the cloth.

She didn't think that Leaf's reaction could be worse than Moonbeam's or Jayda's. It was a heaven place;

why wouldn't Leaf love it? Why wouldn't she love Fannilea more for making it? Too bad, she would know later, that she did not yet understand much about what it meant to be human.

CHAPTER NINETEEN

Leaf didn't smile. She didn't ask questions. She sat, blank-staring. Her eyes put Fann in mind of a crow who has not found food in too many day-risings.

A sinking feel filled Fann's stomach. Too late, she thought she knew something. "You wanted to do it, didn't you? On your own?"

Leaf's eyelids flickered. "Or with you," she said slowly. "But yes. I wanted to ... why did you?"

"Kek. I wanted to help. I wanted you … to like me."

"Is that why you've been doing all this stuff? You're driving everyone nuts."

"Yes! Why so much not-like?"

"They want to know why you're doing it. What you want in return."

A shame-flush gripped Fannilea's lungs. She did not say "nothing" to Leaf.

"It makes people suspicious. If you don't get anything out of it, it's like … it makes them owe you. If you're getting something out of it, then it frees them. It's a trade. Your thing that you want for their thing that they want. Always paid in full, never lopsided. They don't have to wonder if they owe on an unspoken claim. When you say you do it for nothing, they wonder. Everybody has to live, and living means wanting stuff and acting on the wants. You see?"

"They want me to … ask for something?"

"No, it's … more like you already *are* asking for something, by giving them something. They want you to be open about what you're asking. So they can choose to trade or not."

"What if I wasn't? What if I wanted nothing?"

"Only dead people don't want anything."

Dead people and the Murder, Fannilea thought. But that was not true. The Murder tried to say they didn't want, but they did. Order, obedience, faith. Shek. Only they made it having-to, which made it hurt. Here, there was no having-to. The humans got to choose. Wasn't that why she'd come?

Fannilea offered to undo the garden work, but Leaf told her not to.

Fannilea didn't know what to do. She thought-wondered how it would happen if she said to the house members, "I trade gift-giving and meal-finding for you to accept me." It felt not-right, too, but she didn't know why. Also she didn't know if that counted as talking about the contract.

More and more not-right things she did because of that paper. Had the Morrigan tricked her into dealing with the humans the wrong way?

Then there was Slate. Always, there was that iron-eyed one. She had trouble keeping him from her thoughts. Or her thoughts from him, maybe.

She checked the crow trap every day, but still she wanted to give more. Her gifts did not go nice with him. They made him eyeball her more. It was like Leaf said, maybe. Should she stop?

But she had not much time. She could not let the contract run out without doing everything she could. Action, she must take.

She climbed the stairs, not-knowing what she might do. Look-see, wondering about Slate.

At the first floor landing, she stopped. His room was here, below hers. She drifted down the hallway, past the others' rooms, listening.

Quiet, there was. Not many in the house, if any. Slate had gone; she didn't know where.

Magic, it held, the place where he nested. What if she went in? What could she learn? Helping was not working, but was there something else …?

House rules said no. She didn't like to break these. Good for living together, not like the Murder. Sneaking a lot, she had been, for her helping, and she didn't like that, either. She didn't want to hide. She wanted to be like the house members, straight and true.

How could it be right to be what she hated to escape the same thing she hated? It felt so not-right.

But what else was there to do? Defy the Morrigan? Not possible.

For now, she must do. When she was free, it would be better. She could be however she wanted.

She pushed open the door to Slate's room.

A human-sized bag like Fann's puffy coat lay crumpled in one corner; Slate nested on the floor, like Leaf. Stonelike blocks, stacked, with one big wood-piece on top, made a desk. A laptop computer and a framed photo sat atop it.

Faded and ripped, the photo showed a woman and a boy in front of a falling-apart house. Fannilea pinchy-peered at it. The boy stood laughing, mouth falling open, with thunderous eyes.

With a jolt, Fann realized she recognized that laughing boy, barely. It was Slate.

The looks-age of the boy in the photo made her think it must have been taken three or four human-years ago. But the spirit-age of that boy had twice as many years of youth as her iron-boy did now.

The woman smiled with hushed sureness, holding tight to the boy's arm. She had beauty like a warm cup of tea. Smooth and brown, she was—her skin, her hair, her eyes. Only lips shone petal pink, and a scarlet flower tucked behind her ear flashed red.

Happy people with no cares, these two.

This was not-like the Slate she knew. Butter and soft wax, he was here, not flint and rock. What changed?

Was this woman part of it? Twenty years more than him, she had, and her nose and lips bore the same curves. His mother?

Fannilea bumped the desk so-light with her hip, and the machine-brain, next to the photo, lit up. Laptop, Fann reminded herself.

A message showed on its face.

Rafa, please. I just want to see you. Tell me where you're living. Mamá

Underneath, a gray rectangle said REPLY.

Oh the thought Fann had, right-out. She should not do it. It was not her thing to do.

But … she knew about people with pretend-faces, and Slate's mother was not one. She felt true.

And … Fannilea picked up the photo. Such a happy place. How could it go so not-right?

What if it could be fixed? What if Fannilea could help? Shouldn't she? If she brought him back together with his beautiful mother, he would have to accept her. Not-liking-of-crows be kekked.

She clicked the gray box. Her human-heart didn't like it, and turned away, but her crow-heart urged her on. Quick as hops, she pecked out four numbers and three words. More than that, she could not do. She did not wait or reconsider; in that moment it seemed the only thing.

She clicked SEND.

CHAPTER TWENTY

The next day-rising, Fann awoke to Leaf calling her name from downstairs. Yawning, she hop-stepped down to the living room to find the whole house gathered around the most dead-alive skinny-spindly pine tree she had ever seen.

"Moonbeam found us a Christmas tree," Scrap said, grinning. "Ain't it great?"

"Um," Fann said.

Moonbeam plucked at the needle-clumps, trying to fluff. It didn't work. "OK, OK, it's a little bit bare. It'll look better once it's decorated. You're going to help us, right?"

"We don't have lights, but we're making paper and popcorn chains, and Leaf got some tinsel," Jayda said.

"Slate's in charge of the star," Leaf said.

Leaning against the wall behind the tree, Slate made a face at her, but it had play behind it.

"What is the meaning of it?" Fannilea asked.

"The tree? It's pretty," Moonbeam said. "And fun."

"It's a celebration!" Scrap threw tinsel at the tree; only half of it stuck.

A festival, then. Would it be like the Aug? "How does it go? What does it ... celebrate?"

"Us. Life. What we like. Our hard work. What we have because of it." Tinsel dangled from Scrap's fingers, winking in the light. "That it's a great world we live in."

Yes, Fann thought. Yes, it was, and this houseful of semi-lost, scraping-by, scruffy orphans didn't even know quite how much.

Oh, how she wanted to stay here. If not in this house, then at least in this great world.

And so the members of Shady House, including Fannilea Ishika Fiachra, otherwise known as Fann, spent that Christmas Eve afternoon turning that dead-alive skinny-spindly pine tree into a paper-draped, popcorn-topped, star-crowned thing of hope and joy.

Fann hung a popcorn chain, reaching up and around with her left arm and—

"Whoa, that's a wicked scar," Moonbeam said.

Fann dropped both her arm and the popcorn.

"What's it from?"

Everyone stopped mid-decoration.

Fann curled inward. "Broke my elbow," she muttered. "Had to have metal-fixings."

"What happened?"

That remembrance, her first and only riik, and the Boneman, squashed her heart with a stone-fist feel. But she couldn't tell them, not yet. Not until she told them what she was, and that was too soon.

"I ... fell," she said, but her wait-break let them know it wasn't true.

"You don't have to tell us," Moonbeam said.

Fann showed them the half-bend of her arm. "Part-use only. But works well enough."

As an arm it did. Not so much as a wing.

Her greatest fear, when she'd learned it had been broken, was that she would never fly again. Thinking of it, she harsh-breathed, quick and short. Everything that had led to it, so wrong. That riik, wrong, all wrong, nothing but wrong. She had known it, and she had told them, but the Murder hadn't listened.

Chapter Twenty-One

Fannilea Ishika Fiachra had woken with a start.

Something was wrong.

She examined the Ahk. Gray, dead, quietlike, as usual. Murder fast asleep, beaks buried. Nothing different. All well.

Fannilea re-buried her own beak, thinking of sleep, but it came again, that feel.

Something was wrong.

It fluttered into her mind like dark whispers. It tugged on her heart like brokenness of lost-love. Her wings, heavy on her, needed flight.

It called her name.

Her claws fear-danced, light at first and then wild; she almost lost her hold on the branch. On quivering wings, she swooped to the ground and crouched.

A thin mist-curtain fell; Fannilea opened her beak to rawwwk but could not make a sound. Her wings would not make flight; her feet would not walk. Her whole body movement-stopped. Except her heart. That hard-beat so rough she feared it would burst apart.

Dimlike, she knew what this must be, but the teachings had not made her ready for the not-right feel. The teachings had glory-spoken of specialness and honor and the one true meant-to-do. They had not said that she would not be able to control her own self.

Fannilea fought, self-holding, but the mist thickened. The grayness of the Ahk was replaced by a dark, unclean human building with cracked-up windows.

Dark shapes hung everywhere. In front of her, a man sat strapped to a chair, not moving. She couldn't see his face; his head drooped to his chest. The front of his shirt had soaked a deep red that made her chest hurt, and his right ankle bent crooked.

Fannilea didn't like this. A deep wrong-feel gripped her gut.

Then, from beneath her, a pair of arms reached toward the man in the chair. The hands at the end of the arms were big and clumsy with torn-up skin and black hairs on the knuckles. Not hers. But how she saw them, coming up from beneath, reaching out in front of her, made them seem like hers. Whose eyes were these? Whose action was she seeing?

Not her own, that much was sure.

A low moan dragged out of the man. The hands grasped him by the throat and squeezed.

Fannilea thought she might bring up her makeberries.

The man in the chair choked. It looked to Fannilea like *she* was strangling him. She wanted to look away, but she could not; she had no power here.

Even with eyes to close, she would have heard the gagging sounds.

The man in the chair fought, seeking air. But the hands did not let up. They pressed and pressed, until the man's eyes rolled up in his head. He slumped in the chair. Still the hands did not stop.

Fannilea could do nothing but watch.

The hands did not move until there was no more life left in the man.

Then the warehouse disappeared.

Images flew past: those hands again, making a hard crack against the face of a woman with hair like straw and drawings on her skin; a tipsy-topsy-flying-sideways feel behind the steering of a moving-machine, with a narrow miss of the middle-bar of the drive-road; a hammer quick-pounding the fingers of a man in a dim place, one at a time.

Fannilea began to chant the Het Ket Wok Aw Aw. She said it to herself again and again, trying to drown out the thought-stream and worse, the feel of it.

It helped, but not much.

Among the images, one held her. A small girl with caramel skin and a smile full of charm pulled at her—his—sleeve. He knelt and offered the girl a stuffed bear.

Fannilea chanted faster. A daughter? How could such a man have a daughter?

Caught up in the call to riik, she had no heart of her own, only the man's, and yet hers found a way to break.

She kept chanting. More images, more pain.

Another dim-dark place. Crouched behind boxes.

She had a gun in her hand.

Shots echoed. A bead of sweat rolled down her neck, into her collar. The gunfire ceased.

"Boneman!"

That this should be what they called him did not surprise her. She had seen why.

"Come out with your hands up!"

But Boneman had a not-right feeling about that. He would not give up. He would not go to their erawk— their cells.

Boneman burst forward, gun pointing. A bullet punched him in the chest, and his gun clattered to the floor. He clutched his chest, not believing. Never had he believed in death—at least, not for him. It happened to other people, sure, but not to him.

But there it was, a hole in his chest. Dark blood stained his fingers—his blood. He started to shake his head, to fend it off—he stumbled, and fell, and blinked, and stopped moving.

Fannilea jolted back to her crow-self. Her stomach retch-twisted and sent up every last makeberry she'd eaten the night before. A second round brought up nothing but juice. The snapping of finger bones ... she hard-shuddered. She had eyes of her own to close now, but it didn't help—the images were made fast in her mind.

She blinked in the gray light of the Ahk and fluttered her wings, fighting the want of taking off, flying to the human world, hiding. For she knew now, exactly what this was, and she did not want it.

The Ahk lay still. None had woken. Fannilea knew what she must do; there was no use waiting. She opened her beak and sang. The Het Ket Wok Aw Aw sounded to her, for once, like the right and true thing.

It rose in her heart, drawing her crow-family to her. It moved their blood, as it ought. It was shek. They could not resist.

Corley woke and joined his crow-sister with a joy-warble. Manak woke and joined, and then Datchett their chief, and then all were waking and singing and gathering round Fannilea, their white crow-daughter.

Fannilea flew to the tree-top, where she could see all. The teachings had given her made-words for this moment. The first ones, she would follow. But after that ... well. Maybe not.

"Crow-family," she said. "Awoken, I have been, with sight-visions of a man's life and of his death. I have sung you awake so you will know that we have been called to riik."

Fannilea stopped.

The next part, from the teachings, said, *I heart-take the leading of this riik, and I will bring the lost soul safelike from its wanders to the Ahk's edge, where it shall cross to the Otherworld, as is the way of Death.*

Then the Murder would cheer and all would make ready to depart.

This was the start of the ritual of riik, simple. It was their bond; it was their shek.

But Fannilea wasn't going to do it.

"I know I am to heart-take this riik. But this soul ... the one I've been called to path-show ..." She struggled. "He made trouble. He ..."

Flashes of images came. Bones breaking. Fannilea fluffed her feathers, fighting them.

"He was not right. He was a hurter of people. He did not win our help. We should refuse this riik."

Beaks clacked. The Murder-crows jerked their heads to eyeball one another. But they held silent.

"I—I don't heart-take this riik."

Maybe none had ever done this before. Fannilea didn't care. She would not help that hurter. It was not right or true. No matter what shek said.

"Fannilea," Datchett gentled. "There is no such thing as not accepting your riik. You were called. We will go, and you will lead us."

"No," she said. "I refuse."

"Ready yourselves for riik," Datchett called to the Murder. Then he flew to perch beside Fannilea.

"Ock, calm yourself, crow-daughter. You've upset them. I understand your hurt and we must heart-talk. I want to hear your words. But the Murder is more delicate than you. You know that." He hopped close, greased his beak from his oil glands, and set to allopreening her head.

She wanted to get away from him. But she must not hop around like a mad crow. She had to make the right words, to show him, to make him understand.

"What did you see?" he asked.

"This man! He's stuck-mad and mean-bodied and hurt-driven. No sorry feeling. He thinks—"

"I did not ask what you ended on because of what you saw. I asked what you saw."

"I was in his mind! I felt his feelings."

"We will take that into account. First, tell me what you *saw*."

Harsh-breathing, Fannilea told of the terrible scenes she had seen. Her head ached with it.

So. Much. Bone-breaking.

"All right, all right," Datchett said. "The first call to riik is not easy. On mine, I felt the same way."

"You did? You refused your riik?"

Datchett *aw-aw*ed, softlike. "No. I heart-talked with my awoah, and he helped me see that I was wrong. I was called to truth-see the life of a man who had been the starter of a computer-things company. Head in some project, always. Always lost in some invention! His wife and mother were lonely, not-noticed. Three nestlings, left to grow without their father. He made many dollars, and he bought flashy things. Traded those for time with his people.

"A terrible man, he was.

"But when I spoke with my chief, he asked me the same as I asked you—what I saw. There were other things. Those nestlings were well-fed and healthy and had much that other young ones don't. On some few weekends, he played made-up games with them. At night before he went away, he often told them special stories for sleeping. He stopped work to care for his heart-friend when she fell sick. His wife, he made young again with laughter when he did finally come around her. There were things like this.

"It was not as much as I would have wished, maybe, but there was another side to the man's story. There is always another side. What is the other side of Boneman's story?"

"What is there, ever, that makes right a life of finger-breaking?"

Datchett head-butted her neck. "Tell me what else you saw."

Slowlike, Fannilea spoke of the little girl.

"You see? Another side. Think of his daughter when we fetch him. What would she want for him?"

Shifty-footed, this made Fannilea. Could that be right? Use the girl's young sunny cleanness to make-right the man's doings and beings? Could one moment of good-doing make-right a life of being a hurter?

"Our role is not easy, Fannilea. We are called to have faith. That is harder for some of us than others, but you must hold strong. I know … you've had a different sort of nestlinghood. Your parents … I'm sure they had their reasons. But this is your chance to prove yourself. To show the others what you're made of. To truly become one with the Murder."

"This isn't about me."

"Of course it is! It's the open window to make-use of your different spirit and buzzlike energy in a right and true way. This is what you were made for, Fannilea."

She eyeballed him with hard doubts.

"Crow-daughter, you must learn to set aside your own thoughts and feelings. It is not for us to judge. Leave that to the gods. We are born to path-show, and that is all."

Shifty-footed, still she felt. There were things she knew, and they meant things. She did not think she could ignore that.

Plus ... if she heart-took the riik, she would have to twine with the Boneman's soul, so he wouldn't get lost on the way. Danger-filled, it was, and she didn't trust that finger-breaker. How could she?

"What happens to him if we don't go?"

"That is not an option."

"But what would happen?"

"It's not our way, Fannilea. We are made to lead souls on riik. Therefore we do. Always."

"Do you even know what happens? You never tried it, did you?"

Datchett speedy-blinked.

"If the Murder always does it, then you've led people like Boneman before, haven't you?"

Datchett clicked his beak. He had stopped allopreening her. "The ones with the most weighty soul-burdens are the ones most apt to get lost."

"But the Boneman wasn't burdened. He didn't care. He did whatever he thought would work for him in the now. He didn't look for right, or truth."

"We are not here to decide questions of truth." Datchett preened his own wing, deliberatelike, smoothing a not-working spot.

"I watched him break every finger on a man's hand, one at a time. I heard the screams. That is true."

"Perhaps the Boneman had this done to him as a young person. Or worse."

"Does that make-right? Does that mean he has won our help?"

"He does not have to win our help. We help. It is our way." Datchett's black eyes flared fire-bright.

"I wonder if you would think differently if they were *your* fingers?" Fannilea low-spoke, but she did not expect a meaningful answer.

Later, she would think of this and shake her head at how much she had not known that she knew.

"Caught up in mind-bending puzzles, you are. It is silly. You are Kaa. You are called to riik. You will lead."

"Can he … can a soul … hurt us?"

Me, she thought. Can he hurt me, because I'm the one he'll be twined with.

"Of course not," Datchett said, smoothlike. "They don't have bodies."

"They must have a form of some kind."

"Still, they can't hurt us."

"How do you know?"

"Fannilea," Datchett said, a bother-sound in his voice-tone. "I am your awoah. Have faith in me. Have faith in your role. Trust your shek."

Believe. Do not ask questions. Do not look for the thing to make you understand.

She could not. She needed to *know*.

Datchett tossed his head. "Consider this: What if you're right?"

Fannilea blinked.

"How will the Murder get to understand? You know how they are. Need to be shown everything, they do. What if … what if change could be had? By showing?"

Fannilea wondered. Could the Murder change? "If they met the Boneman … ?"

"Might be they would see and understand and take your view."

The white crow stretched her wings. It was not something that had come into her mind before. This blessed tribe never made a new thought … or did it? Could she get them to?

"But what about shek? Shek never changes. Shek is."

"I will tell you an awoah secret, Fannilea, my crow-daughter, for your ears only, but you must blood-swear not to tell the others, not one, not in your life. Will you keep this knowledge close and never give it away? Will you be its guardian?"

Fannilea nodded, and Datchett hopped close.

Lowlike, he said, "Sometimes shek changes, when it's useful."

It was madness. Fannilea preened a wing, thinking. Should she do this thing?

He had not shown her it was not dangerous, which meant it was. The Boneman could hurt her. But … what if the Murder saw? What if they would change?

Worth it, that was. She clacked her beak.

"All right," she said. "I'll do it."

The Murder waited, tidylike.

Jangle-harsh and snappy-sharp, Fannilea's nerves were, but now she must lead. She opened her beak and sang. The Het Ket Wok Aw Aw tribe-held them and made them ready. Datchett joined, and then the rest. Some part of Fannilea upswelled with a pridelike feeling—that she could do this.

With the song soaring, she let go of the branch and dove into the gray light of the Ahk. The Murder left the tree as one, a mist of cinders, as if it rained upside-down from deep inside the earth. Fannilea flew stark at their front, white against black. They followed her true, for once and only.

When the Murder flew into the human world, a heavy boom sounded somewhere far-off, on the other side of the sky. Their wild black cloud burst apart. Here they flew looselike, clustered, trying not to show what they were, but it made no difference.

Below, people stared and pointed.

Fannilea knew what they said. An omen, terrible-like. Death's tread, walking.

How she hated it.

She did not want this fate.

But her sight-images of the Boneman showed her the way. She followed, and before long she saw lights below. Far apart at first, they soon spread gold across the land below.

It left Fannilea without breath.

"Filthy place squished with humans and vermin. We won't have to stay long," Datchett said.

Fannilea had never seen a big city. As humans the Murder lived in a smaller town that told their legend in whisper-breaths and didn't inquire about wrong-things, a place where the Murder was known and let-be, if not exactly accepted. The few riiks she'd been on as a nestling had shown her nothing like this.

Dirty down below, it might be, but above it glittered.

For the first time, Fannilea Ishika Fiachra wondered what it might be like to live as a human. For true and always. She knew she was different from her crow-family; her feathers left that much not-doubted. But she thought she would make it work. It was in her blood, was it not?

But that night, soaring over soft-glow lights, a want began to grow. For that moment, Fannilea tucked it into the back of her heart.

The Murder dove down into dim-dirty buildings covered in paint-pictures. Fannilea led them through a jagged-piece window.

The Boneman was there.

His murky soul-feel touched Fannilea's mind. Heavy and wet, it weighed on her. She clenched her beak and held strong against it.

Fannilea guided her crow-family to the other side of the building, where the Boneman was not. There, the Murder changed as one. From a black-feathered cloud of wild to a people-group, oddlike, in black shifts, it was done in an eye-blink of hurt.

Across the building, a thing made of shadow hung in the air.

"Boneman," Fannilea said. She meant to shout, but the word whisper-fizzled.

The shadow-thing paid her no mind.

Fannilea harsh-swallowed. Datchett nudged her shoulder.

"Boneman!"

This time, the word echoed, bouncing off high ceilings. This time, the soul turned toward Fannilea. She fought to stay right and true before it.

Though he was dead, the Boneman looked as he had in life. His broad, flat face was pocked with pitted scars. His nose angled not-right in two places. Deep eye sockets held two black points with no thought-life in them.

A prickle-feel danced down the back of Fannilea's neck. The hairs on her arms stood up, and her stomach tight-wrung itself. Fly away, she wanted to, right then, more than anything.

But the whisper-chatter behind her said, *Go on.*

"Boneman," she said. "We are the Kaa, and we have come to take you home."

The shadow rushed her. Her gut-thoughts said to step back quicklike, but she thought-stopped them and stood her ground. A beak's width from her face, the shadow stopped.

A question-look developed on the Boneman's face, and then a troubled frown. His dark gaze traveled from side to side and up and down, onto Fannilea and the Murder behind her, and then away. Confusion filled his soul-feel; Fannilea felt it in her heart and knew his pain.

He needed to be taken away from here; he needed to find his rightful place. She would be the one to help him go. It was shek.

Fannilea rattled her own head, shaking it hard. That was not-right. She was here to make the Murder see the true Boneman. She must take care.

"Something is different," the soul said. It raised its shadow hands to eye level and waved them about as though they were odd as wings.

"You've changed," Fannilea said. "You are you but not you. This is not your world anymore."

"Who are you?"

"We are your soul guide. We have come to take you on to the next place, where you belong now."

"Take me to my daughter. That's where I belong. With her."

"Not anymore. You would only be a haunt to her. How would she be happy? No, she must go on without you—and you must go on without her. To a new home, a place that will suit you as you are now."

"Where is this place? Are there others like me there?"

Truth, Fannilea didn't know. The teachings hadn't included answers to questions. In the few riiks she had joined, the souls hadn't asked. The Murder stood behind her, blinking and waiting, more like crows than humans. Datchett offered nothing. So Fannilea did the only thing she could think of—she made it up.

"Of course, lots of others like you. Like a festival."

"Breakable?" the shadow said, a wishlike sound in his voice-tone. "Are they?"

With a stone heart, Fannilea thought of the first man from her sight-images. Slumped in the chair, head down. He had been breakable.

But maybe this was the key. Maybe if she could get him to talk about this, the Murder would see the Boneman's real-self true.

Fannilea took a harsh-breath. "Do you like breaking things? Would you ... like to break them?"

"Oh yes," he said, with a child's want. He slip-slid closer. The air around his mouth smelled of old bones, as if he'd been eating the dust of his gone years.

"Have you broken many, in your time?"

The Boneman-shadow didn't answer. A chill swept over the Murder-crows as one.

"Fannilea," Datchett said. "He is ready."

But Fannilea was not. "How many did you break? Who were they? Tell them. Show them as you showed me, so they will know that this is not—"

"We must go!" Datchett cried.

On his flash-signal, the Murder shifted, bones breaking, hands, arms, legs disappearing in a flurry of feathers, beaks, claws. Fannilea didn't want the change, not now, but her blood cried that she must, and it came, whether she willed it or not.

As Fannilea's change began, the Boneman reached for her. Panic-feel closed her throat.

Nothing-fingers twirled into the space where her human heart had been an eye-blink before, the same space where now her crow-body tried to form ... and she felt him.

Her stomach—was it crow or human or crow or human—made itself fistlike. He had his fingers in her ... space. She didn't know what she was. She didn't know what he was. The wrongness! Burst apart, she would—had she?

She fought to hold, crow, human, but could not find either, only a dull, wide-spaced hurt, everywhere.

The fingers dug deeper, and a whine built around them, keening. Was it her? What was she? Pain-scrabbled. Low-formed. Not-here.

"Breaking . . ." the Boneman hissed.

Almost-crow . . .

His form snapped tight around her wing. A loud crack ripped the air. The Murder yelled.

Noise pressed on Fannilea, coming from nowhere. The Boneman's pressure lifted, but the world tilted, askew.

Dazed, she jerked her head toward where she thought the Murder was. Where were they?

"Cor?" Black dots swam before her eyes. Was that the Murder?

A voice called her name. Manak? Shouting. Where?

"Can you move your wing?"

Her wing? What a silly question. Of course she could move her wing. She stretched out her right wing. There, see? And then, the left.

Except, no. The left one … no. The going, it wasn't. Not … wok?

Someone gentle-pushed. Fingers, a human hand. Her wing bent, and Fannilea screamed, and everything went black.

Fannilea's left arm burned. At the site of her elbow, like a wild-blazing bonfire stoked with dry brush, it ate her alive. Next to that, the dull-flamed ache of her chest mattered hardly. Felt like someone had stuck a tree branch down there and stirred, it did, but oh that arm! On top of that, mind-fog thickened her head and wrenched at her eyelids, wanting to keep them down.

She pushed at the fog; she had to put out the flames in her arm. She looked down.

She did not have an arm. She had a three times bigger white blanket-like thing. She tried to lift it—too heavy. She scratched at it; it was hard and rough, not blanket-like, but stone-like. Something man-made, then, to keep her arm from bending.

The burning persisted, that bonfire in her bones, leaping higher as her mind cleared some. She had an arm, not a wing. She lay in a bed, not on the ground. The walls around her were white, and the sharp stink of no-germ stuff lived in the air around her.

Bad, it must be. The Murder never used human hospitals—too dangerous. Only when there was no other choice would they risk it.

Had she almost died?

The last moments of the riik rushed back. The Boneman-shadow reaching for her. His hissing voice. The feel of his nothing-fingers twisting in her. The cracking sound, sharplike.

The way her wing had turned, against-right ... bile rose. She tried to breathe bigger, to be calm.

Once, when she was a nestling, staying in the human world, she had seen a crow with a broken wing. It tried to hop, but could barely lift itself. There had been a rabbit body, killed by cars, on Fannilea's side of the road; the crow sat huddled on the other. If he could cross, he would have dinner. But how long would it take him? Plus he might be hit himself. And if, with some luck, he did make it? He would have this meal, but what about the next?

Knowing this, she crossed and scooped the crow up. He spoke to her with a low croak. As she set him down next to the rabbit and he began to pick, she thought, at least he's free. Without flying, dead in a few hours he would be, but free.

Manak's voice rose in the hallway.

"She hasn't woken yet; don't you think—"

Datchett bounced into the room, snappy-sharp. Manak followed, low-faced, but he made-happy when he saw her.

"You're awake!" He scurried to her bedside to nuzzle her and drag his fingers through her hair. Crowlike in his love-showing, Manak had always been.

"We were worried," Datchett said.

Fannilea wasted no time. She needed to know. "Will I fly again?"

They eyeballed each other. They both spoke at once.

"I'm sure this is hardly the time for—"

"Fannilea, why don't we make sure you're—"

"Stop." She put up her hand. "Answer the question."

Manak chewed his lip. "Doctors say there's a good-look for your arm to make-right."

An ugly stone-feel sucked at Fannilea's lungs. "But?"

"But … it was broken bad, roughlike, and they think it might not … come all the way."

"What does that mean?"

Manak shrugged.

"We won't know until you heal," Datchett said, gentle as could be.

It was not a no. There was a chance. She might fly again. And maybe …

"Did they see?"

Datchett and Manak eyeballed each other again.

"Did who see what?" the awoah asked.

"The Murder. They saw what the Boneman did. To my wing. To me. When I tried to twine with him."

"Yes," Datchett said.

"Then they know."

Blank eyes, Manak had, while Datchett frowned.

"They saw what kind of person he was," she tried.

"You needn't worry, Fannilea," Datchett said. "It is taken care of. All is well."

Prickle-dots rose on the back of her neck.

"What happened? After?"

"Manak and some of the others brought you here," Datchett said. "I took over the riik."

Fannilea's heart dropped. "You helped him."

"It is our way, Fannilea."

"He broke my wing," she said. "And nearly killed me. On purpose."

Shifty-footed, this made Manak.

"You were the thing keeping him from his daughter. Parents do strange things when someone tries to separate them from their offspring."

Manak gave Datchett one uppity eyebrow. Maybe he thought of Fannilea's own true parents, who did not seem to mind being separated from their daughter.

"You said he was ready!"

"Someday you will understand."

"You think it's okay that he broke my wing. That I'm supposed to accept that, too. Should I die for shek, as well as lose parts of myself?" I might never fly again, she thought, and avoided looking at the stonelike blanket on her arm.

"Sometimes we must make difficult choices to fulfill our duty. It is what it is. It is our blood-life. Perhaps you've learnt from it? Next time you will not question your shek."

Fannilea's mouth dropped open. "You never meant for them to see, did you? Only for me to do your must-do."

She didn't need his answer; she knew it was true.

She should have known. For Datchett followed shek, and none could be apart or different or alone under shek. Only together.

That was when Fannilea knew she must escape. By any means necessary.

CHAPTER TWENTY-TWO

"I almost forgot!" Scrap crowed, snapping Fann out of thought-memory.

"We were hoping you would." Jayda hung a shiny red ball ornament on a thin branch.

"Oh, c'mon, you weren't going to remind me?" Scrap squawked with mock wounds. "Just for that, I'm going to sing three times louder. And I'll sing three times as many rounds."

"What? What did you forget?" Fann asked, but she had a dive-down feeling that she already knew.

"It's tradition!" Scrap started to sing at the top of his lungs. *"Here's a story of a house named Shady, which was full of three very lovely girls …* hmm. A rewrite's in order now that Fann's joined us."

"She hasn't finished her trial," Slate said.

"Yeah, but—"

"It's all right, Scrap," Fann said. "You can sing it the way it is for now."

Scrap started over.

Fann waited for the song to work. Now that she'd been around the house a while, it ought to affect her … right? Without thought, she held her hands to her ears. If it were like the Het Ket Wok Aw Aw, that wouldn't help, but her human deep-feels had begun to take over, and sometimes she couldn't help herself.

"Aw, man," Scrap said. "I guess Fann hates it, too."

Jayda and Moonbeam giggled, look-sharing.

"Oh no!" Fann said, dropping her hands. "It's not that. It's … I didn't want it to have power over me."

Silence fell.

Had she offended them? She needed them to know more about her, soon. Might as well begin to try. "This song is not meant to bind you, is it?"

"Bind us? Like a spell?"

"To … keep you tied. To each other."

"We're friends," Scrap said. "We choose to be bound. But … the song is just a silly thing I made up. Have you seen that old TV show *The Brady Bunch*? I guess not. The song is a rewrite of the show's theme song."

"What about the name? Shady?"

"He picked that because it rhymes," Moonbeam said.

"It's also appropriate," Scrap grumbled.

Fann frowned. "Not many trees by the house."

Jayda snorted. "Not that kind of shady. It also means dubious. Not trustworthy. A bit dark."

"That's what makes it perfect!" Scrap crowed. "Are you gonna tell me that we're NOT a shady bunch?"

Jayda threw a pillow at him.

Scrap let it hit him in the face. "You all are not nice. Here I compose a sweet little ditty to celebrate our friendship and all you give me in return is mockery and pillow blows. I do not even believe it. Hmpf."

A squawkish giggle escaped Fann before she could stop it.

"Sing with me!" Scrap pulled at her arm.

Moonbeam led with a high, ice-crystal voice.

After a moment's hesitation, Fann warbled her way into the song, too.

Suspicious at first, she soon gained a good-feel. It was not like the Het Ket Wok Aw Aw. As she sang, her brain fizzed, but only with warm-heart, not with the fog of must-do. No filling of her thoughts with theirs, only a happy-feel, all her own.

Shady House was not a Murder. Just a people house trying to make it work by free choice. She wanted to stay, of her choice, too. They had a right and true thing.

The only problem here was her.

The doorbell rang, and Fannilea quailed.

Everyone stopped singing.

"Is someone expecting guests?" Leaf asked.

Fannilea's crow-heart thudded hard.

"I'll get it," Scrap said. "At least I'm not head-to-toe in tinsel and popcorn, like the rest of you delinquents." He disappeared down the hall.

Moments later, a strangled cry rose from the direction of the front door. The house members chased after Scrap.

"Scrap?"

"What happened?"

"Who is it?"

They ended in the doorway in a clump of limbs, all trying to see over each other. Fannilea slipped in along the wall and peered through slitted eyes.

A woman stood in the doorway—the woman from the photograph on Slate's desk. Not that Fannilea would have known that if she hadn't been expecting her. She had the same warm café mocha skin, but after only a short time since then, her eyelids hung heavy and low, and her skin sagged and wrinkled. Her pupils loomed large and burned with a dark light. Her hair hung in greasy strings.

The happy-faced young woman of the photo had gone. This was a different-inside person, just like Slate.

"Rafa?" she asked with a touch of not-sure.

"Mamá?" Slate exploded through the barrier of the others.

Fann kept out of his way.

"What are you doing here? How did you find me?"

"But …" she said. "You wrote to me."

Slate didn't answer. He spun, iron-eyes blazing, back to the house members. His gaze fell on each until he got to Fann. On her face, the fire went out and his eyes returned to flat.

"You," he said. "This is your doing."

His voice-tone clanged with metal, too. Immovable. Dead, with no hope. A pain that cannot be reached. Better it would be if he squawked and scolded.

But this … she had done wrong. Why had she thought it would be OK?

He was waiting for her to speak.

Fann could not lie to him.

"Yes," she whispered. "I thought …" But she didn't know what she'd thought. She wanted to impress him; she wanted to impress them all.

"What did you do? How did you know?"

"Rafa—" Slate's mother tried, but he held up his hand and kept his focus on Fannilea as she stumbled around her words, trying to find the right ones.

She could not defend herself. The thing she had done was not right and true, whatever the Murder said. She had agreed to good rules and not followed them. She would have to take her punishment. From the set look on her iron-boy's face, it was going to be the end of everything.

"I ... went in your room. I bumped the desk and the computer was on. I saw her message." Fannilea's throat hurt. She wanted to explain, but how could she when she couldn't talk about the contract?

"So? You thought you'd play a joke?"

"No! It was serious. I ... wanted to help."

Kekking stupid, it sounded. What right did she have? Meddle, is what she did. Like the Murder member she was. Like every stupid crow. No wonder he hated them so. She hated herself.

"You went into my room without asking. You looked at my messages. And then? Your fingers slipped and you sent my mother my address, by accident? And you thought this would be okay, because you wanted to help me? Am I getting this right?"

Fannilea closed her eyes. There was nothing to say.

"You've been nothing but a busybody since you came here. All you do is stick your nose in everyone else's life. You don't respect the house. You don't belong here. I made a terrible mistake letting you stay. This is the end of your trial. Now. Get whatever things actually belong to you and get out."

Somehow her crow-heart had known that this was what must happen, but it crushed her human-heart to hear it all the same.

She clutched the wall. Her elbow-metal pressed hard against the inside of her skin. She knew by looking at him that she would not be able to talk him out of it. It was no use even trying.

His iron-eyes held no feeling; a stranger, she was, to him. Less, because she'd made herself his enemy.

She would have to go.

She let go of the wall. Slate's mother's eyes lowered, full of sorry. Fann stepped toward the door.

"Fann, wait," Leaf said. "Just wait. There are things you'll want to take with you." Her voice wobbled. "And … Slate," she whispered, her mouth drawn in hurt. "It's Christmas Eve. Couldn't she …"

"No. No more. It's done. She broke the house rules. She lied. To you. To me. To all of us. She doesn't belong here. She never did."

"But ..."

"Enough. She'll get her things—and only her things —and leave. Tonight."

Chapter Twenty-Three

She was cast out.

These people would never accept her now. Not even as human, let alone as her true Kaa self, as the contract wanted. Oh how she wished she could go back in time. Back to that kekking moment in front of the computer. Move away from the desk—leave it!

Fannilea sat on the floor of her room, cross-legged, shoulders lowlike. Leaf had refused to let her leave without a pack, but she had needed to escape the presence of that iron-boy. The way he did not see her hurt too much.

Repurposed rubbish, her whole life was. The home she had hoped for had shattered under her nosy beak. What of that would she want to drag along to make her remember the hurt even more? Nothing. She didn't want to take a thing from Shady House; it would mean she wasn't coming back.

Besides, if she could not win this contract, she was dead. Dead-alive in the Murder or dead-for-true by the Morrigan's hand if she would not go back.

The white-feathered mask on the wall, that she might take. Somehow it had become hers. A symbol of the home she almost had.

A gentle knock sounded on the doorjamb.

Leaf stood in the doorway, twisting a piece of nesty hair around a finger. A black pack hung from her other hand. Her dark eyes loomed wild and large, like a spooked thing.

"I packed you some clothes ... some food, but you do pretty well for food on your own, I guess ..."

She broke and tried again.

"Fann ... what happened? I thought you would ... I don't know. It was like you were a different person once you were in the house."

Fannilea harsh-breathed. This was it.

This was the moment. She had to do it.

When she blood-dripped on that contract, she had been full of not-sure. How would she do this? She did not know. But here now, her human friendy was asking her for truth.

This, Fann could do. Not the contract, no—but the rest. Who she was. A little right truth, for Leaf to know. Fann would make it more even, this way.

Leaf had fought for her. She had offered her a true home, brought her into Shady House despite the not-usual about Fann. She had seen through the weird and the wrong-ways to who Fann tried to be—past the crow-heart to the human one.

That was something.

Fann would trade Leaf truth, for what the chickie-lion girl had already given. This was the real help Fann could give.

"Leaf," she said. "Come here. I must tell you something."

Leaf set the pack down and perched on the floor next to Fannilea. She showed no signs of questions. Only a quietlike waiting, like she had fore-known. Fannilea wondered how many humans were like this girl Leaf. She thought not many.

"Do you know of an ancient people called the Kaa?"

"No. Should I?"

"Not before now, no. There are tales told of them in the Southwest, where crows are many, but mostly they are not spoken of. It is how it ought to be."

"Crows?"

"They are a secret race that changes shape. Mostly, crow. Sometimes, human."

"A myth, then."

"No. Real."

"A secret race of crow-people," Leaf said. Doubt coated her voice-tone.

"Yes."

"Where do they live, when they are human?"

"Sometimes, here."

Leaf's liquid look turned pointy. "Here? *Right* here?"

But Fannilea knew there was only one way to prove what she had to say next. So she didn't say a word. Instead, she changed.

Leaf blinked and blinked like a crow herself.

There on the floor, in a little heap of feathers, where her friend had been a moment before, now sat a white crow with big blue eyes and a crooked wing.

"Fann? That's you?"

The bird croaked and hopped closer, her gaze meeting Leaf's with uncanny intelligence.

Leaf leaned over and laid her hands, cupped together, on the ground. The crow hopped in. Leaf raised her to eye level and held her delicately.

"Wok," the crow said.

"Wow," Leaf muttered. She stared at the bird in her hands, considering. "You know," she said finally. "This explains a lot about you."

The crow nipped her thumb.

Leaf laughed. "Not in a bad way. It's just that it makes sense. There were a lot of things that didn't. So there's more of you? And you've left them?"

The crow bent her head way down over Leaf's hand. Her tail feathers rose up. She dove, letting go, and flapped crookedly to the floor.

In an eye-blink, Fann the human girl with the spiky hair and blue eyes once again sat before Leaf.

"Wow," Leaf said again. "So that's you. The real you. The white crow."

"*This* is the real me," Fann said, gesturing at her human body. "Whatever they are, I don't want to be."

She told Leaf of the Kaa—their home in the Otherworld, their role as soul guides, the Murder, shek. Even her first riik, all about the Boneman—she shuddered when she thought of his sunken eye sockets —and what had happened to her arm. She had not spoken of this before. But she laid it out for Leaf as best she could. Her decision to escape. Then, the doing of it. Her choice of Shady House as a place to rest, no more.

The only thing she didn't tell her about was the contract. Instead she said, "This is why it mattered so much to me to make a home here. I wanted to do it the best way, but I didn't know what that was. I went the wrong way. I am sorry."

Right and true, it was, this telling. Bone-deep, she felt it, more than anything since she'd left the Murder. It felt like herself. Even if it hadn't been for that kekking contract, she would have told Leaf these things. Self-right, it was, not shek-right. She would not regret it, no matter what Leaf said.

"I need to think," Leaf said, twisting her hands.

Fann fought the clouding of her hearts.

"It's all right," Leaf said. "It is. I just … I want to go for a walk. Will you stay and talk more when I get back? Tell Slate I asked you to. I … I'm glad you came here. I … this won't have to change our friendship."

Leaf sounded not-sure, but Fann would take it— acceptance, it was. Or, it would be, soon enough.

"It's not going to change even one thing between us," Leaf said.

Fann hoped it would be true.

CHAPTER TWENTY-FOUR

Outside of the red brick house in the human city, all lay quiet. No one would know, from eyeballing, that something not-right was happening inside. Unless, of course, that someone happened to be not-quite human. If that someone might take the shape of a wire-skinny black-feathered crow, then he might fly up to the third-floor windowsill of a certain window of that self-same house just in time to witness this not-right thing.

A crow-sister, changing in front of a human! As a show! It could not be believed. Hadn't she done enough against shek?

Corley Drust Fiachra heffed, feathers bristle-burly. How could she? It was not done!

Kaa were not to tell. Kaa were secret. It was the way.

He kept far and voice-stopped his squawks. Full of care, he must be. Blacklike, most of his feathers were, but there were those kekking white stripes, and his crow-sister had keen seeing. She must not know he was here. Too late, it was, to stop what had happened. But there could be no more. The Morrigan's assurances did not satisfy. Someone had to stop that white-feathered crow-girl.

Feel-close to her, he had, before-ago. But now ...

Now she did not-right by her people. She did self-right, not shek-right, and she would have to pay for that. Suffer the end-events, she would. The Murder could only try so hard.

He could only try so hard. He would feel-close no more. Something had to be done, so he would do. But what? How?

Corley settled in on the windowsill. He listened, and he waited. The told-girl said she would walk. This gave him thoughts, and he followed his thoughts.

A swoop off the window ledge, and around the house he flew. In a tree over the street, he perched. There he waited again.

The told-girl came out the door.

She walked, and as she did, Corley left his perch and became a feathered black shadow flying some paces behind. For Corley Drust Fiachra refused to let his crow-sister get in her own way of being saved. She would return, even if he had to make an ugly thing happen first.

CHAPTER TWENTY-FIVE

Worry, so much worry, there was. Something was not-right. More than one human-hour had passed, and Leaf had not come home.

Fannilea hopped downstairs and poked her head out the front door. Snow fell, mushy-fat flakes that made it hard to see. Red-color spread everywhere in the winter world, with an eerie feel that Fannilea did not like.

She did not see Leaf.

She closed the door and hurried through the house. Poking her head out the back door, she peered through the drip-dropping snow at the pine tree.

Empty, it was.

A cold-feel snaked down her spine. Where were the crows?

Before, she thought their here-ness the most terrible thing. But this was worse. Where had they gone? What were they doing?

Why hadn't Leaf come back?

Fann leapt the stairs. On the second level, she clattered down the hall, calling for Slate. She opened the door without knocking and plunged through.

He sat on his bed, shoulders sunk, the photograph from his desk in his hands. He kept his iron-gray eyes on the photo, not-seeing.

"Why are you still here?"

"Leaf went. Walking. Didn't come back. Going to be quick, she said. But so long, it was, and—"

He had his jacket on before she could finish. "I'll find her."

"I'm coming!" she shouted after him.

He didn't argue, just left. She rushed to keep up, grab her coat, hop downstairs, follow him out.

He yanked at his collar, uglylike, as they stepped into the wet snow. Fann pulled up her hood and followed. He turned in the direction of the park.

Snow swirled, hissing as it careened into trees. It made the world quietlike, and if she didn't have a heart so full of worry, it might be pretty. Now, though, it meant more danger, and she wished it would stop.

Kek, how she hated walking. So confusing. Where to put feet? Where to put arms? Stumble-blocks everywhere. Uneven pavement. Tree roots. Her own kekking feet. And with someone! How to know where he would be? How fast or slow? So much bumping into each other.

But as she step-hopped beside this gray-eyed iron-boy, something different happened. The stumbling and the bumping melted. Fannilea, gangly crow-girl, became a graceful thing. Somehow that boy knew the things—where she would be, when, how she would move, even before she knew them.

He kept alongside at a right-pace.

Once, she hit a bump. As she twirled, trying not to fall, he put an arm out. She grabbed, and somehow this arm let her find the place for her foot. She caught herself and kept on, easy.

How right it felt. To her. But his hate, still she felt it, collected on his skin.

"I'm sorry," she said. "I shouldn't have done it. So wrong, I was. I ..."

She wanted to say more, but she could not tell him of her life. He wouldn't hear it if she tried.

He kept his quiet, and they walked on.

Fann shuffled, watching her feet, ducking her head. Slate halt-stopped and yanked her arm.

They had reached the corner of the park. At the other end, lights flashed. Red. Blue. Red. Blue.

Fann's heart leapt hard against her throat.

Slate took off across the white.

The mushy-fat flakes had gone; as she ran, needle-sleet stung Fann's cheeks. Her too-big pants dragged, hems soaking, and she tugged on her hood-strings, trying to keep the wet out, but it didn't care. Her hood soaked through and damped her face.

Two black-and-white cars blocked off a space of road at the other end of the park. Black-and-yellow tape made a big rectangle. A crowd had gathered. A man in navy clothes with shiny things on his shirt, full of puffed-up shoulders, reminded Fann of Datchett with the way he over-looked the crowd, like it was his. Inside the tape, he was. They needed to talk to him, the power-guy.

They crept close, hop-stepping at the crowd-edges. There, the worst thing, a white bus with red stripes, with more lights flashing, turning the fallen snow pink.

Where's Leaf? Fann's throat sting-prickled.

The back doors of the white bus hung open, waiting. A carry-bed lay on the ground in front.

It had a person in it.

Fann crow-stretched her neck. But couldn't tell. Ugly kekking snow was all she could see.

Slate crowd-pushed until the power-guy came forward.

"Stand back, please," he said.

"What happened?" Slate asked.

The man repeated himself, gaze pointy.

Slate took a step back. "Please," he said. "We're ... it might be my friend."

Fannilea's human-heart yearned to touch him, but her crow-heart didn't dare.

The Datchett-clone pinchy-peered at them. After one up-and-down look, he let out a big breath. "Hit and run. Something spooked the driver. Swerved right into the girl."

Couldn't feel her fingers, could she? Would they fall off? Would she care?

"What ... what did she look like?" Her voice worked. Kekking weird.

The man eyed her wet hoodie and too-big pants. "I'm sorry, but—"

He didn't get to finish, because the helper-guys lifted that carry-bed into the air and Fannilea could see.

She could see bushy, gnarly, nesty black hair.

"Leaf!"

Her hands flew forward, reaching. Glass-eyes blocked her.

"Stay back."

"That's her! That's our friend! Her name is—"

Fann realized in that moment that she had no idea what Leaf's real name was.

"Lydia," Slate said. "Her name is Lydia Byrne."

"They're taking her to Woodhull. You can call the hospital. I can't let you past."

"Will she be all right?"

"Call the hospital."

The helper-guys closed the doors of the bus. Fann watched as they climbed in to the front.

How still Leaf had been. So still.

The warning-noises wailed to life. Fann winced, but she did not cover her ears. She listened and watched as the white bus carried her friendy away.

She watched until she could not see that bus, not even a speck of red light in the far-away. Then she turned her eyes to the tape area.

"We have to go back to the house," Slate said, but she barely heard. "I have to call her mother."

"Will she want that?" Fann asked, distracted.

"It doesn't matter. We have to now."

Fann hop-stepped away, close-staring at the street. There, where Leaf had been hit. She didn't see anything yet, but ... she walked, following the tape, eyeballing the ground. She didn't want to miss it ... something, there must be. Some shows-the-truth.

Slate watched, a few paces behind.

Nothing, there was nothing.

Maybe she was wrong ... maybe they wouldn't ... maybe they hadn't ... —but there.

It was on the ground, outside the yellow-black tape, on top of a black plastic bag. They blended so well that she almost didn't see.

A clump. Of something black. And featherlike.

The policeman's words returned. *"Something spooked the driver."*

Kek it. She knew *what* the something was, if not *whom*. One of them. Did it matter which? They were all one, weren't they? All guilty.

Those kekking bastards! How could they?

They would not get away with it.

She would see to that.

Fann inched closer, dallying. No one was watching. In an eye-blink, she squatted, grabbed, and stood— then hurried back toward Slate.

"There's something I have to do." She kept her hand in her pocket.

"What did you find?"

"No time. Have to go. I'll be back soon."

"What? Where are you going? Leaf's—"

"It's important. I know you won't trust, but it is. I will try to explain, soon."

His iron-eyes closed like a falling wall.

Her whole heart wanted to fall apart, but there was no help for it—she had to fight for Leaf now. Iron-boy would have to wait, and if he wouldn't, she would live with a heart broken. If she lived at all.

She spun and fled into the park. Some sliver of her wondered if he might try to stop her. But as she ran, nothing happened, and when she turned to look, unable to not, he had gone.

Would she be able to tell him true? Would he believe her? Would he forgive her?

But she must leave her Slate worries aside for now. She had a Murder to face up with.

CHAPTER TWENTY-SIX

Fannilea Ishika Fiachra flew as she had never flown before. She did not feel the wind, though it seared her feathered cheeks and stung her slitted eyes. She did not notice the ache of her crooked wing, though it slow-burned with the feel of an old hurt. With the clump of crow feathers clutched in her claws, she tore ahead.

Anger is not right and true. It is low and base. Best it is to rise above anger and forgive those who have wronged us.

Fann flew harder. The Murder ... this is what they had taught her. But her own heart said something different. Her heart said that to love hard, you must hate hard. You must hate the thing that would harm the love. You must be willing to protect the loved thing from the thing that would destroy it.

If you could stand by and let it be hurt, how then could you claim to love? Love required action. It required your being there and your ready-to-stand-up-and-fight feel.

The Murder had not taught her these things, yet she knew them.

Fann cared for Leaf. Loved her, even. The Murder could not be allowed to harm her.

Surely the Morrigan would not stand for it. She was the decider of Life and Death. She would not take kindly to the Murder's interference.

The world streamed past in a blur of thought-racing and blood-boiling and heart-raging.

In the Ahk, the Murder perched in the tree, cozied in a clump of black, wrapped in a cocoon of murmur, the sleep of crows untroubled by conscience.

Fann shattered it without sorry-feel. She dove at the tree, crying at the top of her voice. Again and again she dove, shrieking, a Leaf-picture in her mind.

The Murder woke. Blinked and whispered, they did. Their hissy, not-right-telling voice-tones washed over her, and a thought turned clear in Fann's mind.

She did not belong to them.

She held on to it as they chitter-chattered, scolding. Maybe it had been there before? But she had not thought it like this—so true.

So right and true.

Datchett said, "Fannilea? What's happened? You've returned?"

"You hurt Leaf."

The whispers hissed harsher.

Datchett hopped, delicatelike. "Ock, Fann—"

"I want to know who."

Yes, it mattered not. One was like the rest. But Fann could not thought-stop her want to know. It mattered to her. *She* was not like the rest.

She perched at the top of the tree with a scorn-look below. "Make it easy! If you have done a right and true thing, tell us! Bare-talk, do not hide! You should be full of right-feel."

Not a single crow moved.

Fann close-watched. Who was not-meeting-eyes? Who was hop-stepping, delicatelike? Who was guilty?

Manak was not-looking, but that was his self-way. Didn't have the go-do-it-ness, did he? He would wish for someone else to do it, while he hid in the nest.

Surely not Corley ... but he had the ableness. He watched her with a lazy-eye gaze, half-open lids, so she couldn't tell. But he wouldn't. He cared for her. He'd want her back in the Murder, but he wouldn't hurt to get it. A good bird, he was. Still her friend, if less now.

Then again, when she came to meet the Morrigan, hadn't he joined the Het Ket Wok Aw Aw without a thought for her? And if it were true, what she thought about the need for love-fighting instead of sitting back and letting hurt happen, could he truly love her? When had he ever fought for her? Would he now?

"Corley Drust!" she called. "What say you? Was it you? Did you hurt my friend?"

A shrill scream answered her. "How can you ask that of your crow-brother? You have lost your way, white one. I have tried to help you! I have tried."

Dropped his look, he did, but not before Fann saw—what? Something not-right. But what was it? She didn't know. She had not seen such a look on her crow-brother Corley before.

Also there was Datchett—as awoah, he wouldn't go himself, but he might send someone. Helper-crow Pomo or Tek.

Wrede could have. She had played with Corley and Fannilea as nestlings. To draw Cor's notice, might she? With beak high, she gave a pointy glare, not-caring. If she had done it, she thought it good.

The others ... how could Fannilea know? If they thought it shek-right, they would do it. It made no point to wonder-think. She must make them show.

Fann thrust out her leg. There she showed the feathers clutched in her crow-toes. They stuck out, solid-dark against the gray light of the Ahk.

"You don't have to say. I will find out. Show your tail feathers. Someone misses these."

The Murder did not answer her. How unlike them to say nothing.

"No? Datchett? A simple thing, it is."

Datchett made no words.

"The Morrigan and I have signed a blood contract. You have no right to interfere."

"The Morrigan will not intervene in Murder affairs," Datchett said in a frozen voice-tone.

"Why don't we ask her about that?" Fannilea didn't know how to call the Morrigan, but it was clear that Datchett wasn't going to do it for her, so she did the only thing she could think of and made it up.

Stronglike, she said, "I, Fannilea Ishika Fiachra, call upon the Morrigan, decider of battles, goddess of Life and Death, to make-right this matter of feathers."

That ought to do it. She hoped.

All fell still.

Creeping, a new gray mist turned the Ahk heavy. It damped the Murder's feathered cheeks and made it hard to see each crow-brother and sister. After filling the space, the mist came together, forming anew in one spot in front of the tree. There it pulled into a body-shape. Soon the body-shape could be seen as a raven-haired woman. The Morrigan, answering the call.

Fannilea gulped.

The Morrigan shook her hair-mane. "Fannilea Ishika Fiachra, you have called. What is it you seek?"

"The right and true thing for a loved one. The Murder has hurt her, badly. She lies in a hospital bed. Keep her life … she might not." Fann showed the feathers. "I found these at the scene."

"Kaa feathers cannot be told from crow feathers. You know that."

Datchett rushed in with many words. "Lady, it wasn't us. We would not harm our crow-child. It's a happen-stance. A regular crow-bird out for a fly who happened upon Fannilea's friend … you know how crows get when there are Kaa about."

"I do. And so, I believe, does Fannilea."

"They did it," Fann cried. "They must show me their tail feathers. Someone has these missing." She flashed the clutched ones again, determined.

"A reasonable request, perhaps, even without much evidence. Will you agree to it, Awoah Datchett?"

"Certainly, my Lady."

Fann whuffed. So fast? Now? Why? Surely he would not let the do-er be caught. Could they have a plan to hide the missing feathers?

But she had asked and they had agreed.

Each member of the Murder turned about, one at a time, showing her their backside.

Fannilea close-studied each set of tail feathers. She spent long on Corley's and on Wrede's but neither had a single feather out of place. And neither did a single other crow in the whole rest of the Murder.

Not Datchett. Not Pomo. Not Tek. Not Manak. No one. All tail feathers seen and accounted for.

"Are you satisfied, Fannilea?" the Morrigan asked.

Fann had no choice. "Yes," she said, frowning. How had they managed it?

"None of this was called for, Fannilea" Datchett said, smoothlike. "You left us, and that is against shek. We have proved that it was not us who hurt your friend, but even if your Murder *had* tried to return you to us, at any cost, then you still could not say your crow-family was not-right for it. A Murder together is a needful thing. If one had done it, they would only have been right-fighting for themselves—and for you, their crow-sister. All of that is *your* doing. No one else."

Wok? *She* was to be blamed because *they* refused to let her go? Senseless, it was. She did not accept.

"I have brought no harm to you. I have asked one thing: to be left to make my way, self-right, apart. *You* have brought harm to *me*. To my dear one. That is a different thing between us, and it is one I won't forget.

"I renounce the Murder, and I renounce shek. I am done with you."

Whisper, they did.

But Fannilea Ishika Fiachra ignored the crows.

"Lady, a word?"

"You may," the Morrigan said.

She swooped down to the goddess's finger-perch.

"They did this; you must know."

"What am I to do? Your awoah says they didn't. They have shown the feathers."

"It's a lie. They hid it somehow. I know it."

"Be that as it may, the Murder is not under contract to me. You are."

"So they can hurt me and the ones I care for as they please? To stop me?"

"You're the one who wants to escape them," the Morrigan said, and her voice-tone had an oddlike sound that Fann had not heard before—something gentlelike—but it left before she could be sure.

"You could not have expected it to be easy."

The bottom half of Fann's beak quirked, one way, the other, as she fought not to squawk. She had expected more from the Morrigan, and yet shouldn't she have known?

Tricksy gods were not to be trusted.

She was on her own.

"Now take these,"—the Morrigan hung a small pouch round her neck, which smelled of the tang of makeberries—"and beak up, for you must fly back and deal with your human problems. I'll keep an eye on those crows, but I can't promise anything. You will have to defend yourself, Fannilea. And you had best remember that for now, the Murder still considers you one of their own."

"I'm not."

A slow, sad lip-curl spread across the Morrigan's face. "If you believe that, you had better win this contract of ours."

"I intend to."

"And if you don't? What then?"

"There is no if," Fann said. "I will win it."

The Morrigan shook her head, saying nothing.

And Fann, as she took off for the human world, leaving the Ahk behind, had to admit that there was an if. There were a lot of ifs, and any of them could mean contract-fail.

And contract-fail was everything-fail.

CHAPTER TWENTY-SEVEN

Light pink soft-dusted the sky as Fannilea crossed between worlds, and she realized with a snap that day-rising had come.

Now that the rush of her anger had ebbed, her limbs drooped. Flying so furious had taken the last of her strength. So much she had been through, tonight!—Slate's anger, telling Leaf of herself, fearing for Leaf's life, flying out, dealing with the Murder, flying back.

Her crow-body ached with tired. Each time she flapped, her wings fell slower and slower and did not want to rise again. Her eyes drifted closed, and she made them open again. She needed to reach the house. She needed to speak with Slate.

She didn't know what she would say, but there must be something. All the things. Whatever she felt. She would make him listen.

Her lungs flared with pain, and her eyes drifted closed again. She wobbled. Just as she thought she might fly no more, there was Shady House, up ahead. Through slitted eyes, she noticed something off about the garden ... was someone there?

One more flap. A figure, there on the bench.

Another flap, and she knew him.

She jinked left and swooped below his line of sight. It was barely twenty degrees—what was he doing sitting out there?

Her heart lurched.

Did the worst thing happen to Leaf?

She sped face-first down to the front door; changed from crow to human without regard for lookers-on;

and rushed inside and up the stairs to her room, where she threw on a puffy jacket. She took the last two stair-flights at top speed and burst onto the roof.

Slate hardly moved, as though he'd been expecting her.

She tumbled onto the bench.

"How is she?"

"Alive," he said.

Fann let out a relief breath, clutching the bench arm. At least there was that.

"They did what they could. But she hasn't woken. They don't know if she will."

Well, Fann thought. Not great. But better than not-alive.

"Did you talk to her mother?"

"Yes. She came down. She's with her." His voice cracked.

She will wake. She has to.

"Visiting hours are nine to five."

"Right," Fann said, rubbing her eyes. "And I'm to leave the house. But …"

"Fann," Slate said, sounding like he hadn't heard.

The thing he said next made her think he hadn't listened to anything she'd said since she arrived.

"You're one of them, aren't you?"

His voice-tone did not have a go-away-feel—only a sense of what already is and cannot be hidden from.

Fannilea dared only a sideways look.

He kept on. "That's why the crows came back. Because you're one of them. The crow-people."

She saw no iron in his eyes—instead, a lost-ness. It made her miss the metal. At least there was sure-ness, in that.

"You had something to do with it, didn't you? Or they did. That's why you left. Why, Fann? Why would they do it? Why are they so?"

It was time to tell him. Somehow or other, he already knew. She must give him the rest, as he asked.

But she was not nestling-silly enough to think it would go well. Leaf's hurt had left him softlike, but that go-away-feel lived below. Hate did not leave easy.

"Tell me the truth, Fann."

Her left arm had gone numb, and the elbow burned with an ugly ache. She had flown too much today.

"All right," she said. "But only if you will, also."

Surprise flared in his gray eyes. "What truth do I owe you?"

"What did the Kaa do? Why do you hate them so?"

"You *are* one of them, then."

"I was born to them."

He closed his eyes. "I knew it," he whispered.

"But I am not one of them. That's why I'm here. I escaped."

He barked a hard, sharp laugh. "So did the other one, according to *mi papi*. That's how he destroyed my family."

A lightning-feel zipped down Fann's spine. The other one? Who escaped? How could it be? She had never heard of such a thing. But then, the Murder wouldn't like to talk of it, would they? ... especially if it were true.

"There's a ... legend that's shared in my family. It's told to the children when they're young—a tradition, passed down with each generation. But *mi papi*, my grandfather, did not believe the story, and he did not want to tell it to his daughter, *mi madre*. When she was a child, he moved her far from the rest of his family in Chile, and brought her here, where she would never hear the story.

"My mother grew up, married, and had a child of her own, me. But then her grandmother, Papi's mother, Sofia, contacted her, without Papi's knowledge. Sofia was sick, on her deathbed, and she said she wanted to talk to my mother. She said she had important things that needed to be said.

"So my mother paid a visit to Chile. When she returned, she had changed. The happy woman she had been was gone. She didn't care about anything she used to love. She lived in her own head, lost.

"I asked Papi what was wrong. He didn't know how to help. When I told him she'd gone to see Abuela Sofia, he became furious. He would not tell me why— kept saying that his *mamá* had no right.

"My mother became worse. She quit her job and stayed home, doing nothing but daydreaming. Papi tried to talk to her, but nothing he did or said helped. I heard him say to her, 'He's not real. They're not real. You have to stop,' but I didn't know what it meant.

"My mother started drinking. At first I didn't realize; she hid it or did it when I wasn't home. But before long she began to leave bottles lying around.

"She wasn't mean. Sometimes I wished she would be. I wished for her to yell, so I could yell back and break that *silencio muerto* that had fallen over our home. She was only sad, though, never angry. Often she cried for no reason.

"My father stayed away more and more. Papi moved in to help around the house. He made sure I ate and went to school.

"No one was surprised when my father filed for divorce, not even me. I knew how I felt about the way my mother's eyes never quite focused on me, the way she seemed to see right through me even when I sat next to her and held her hand. If I could have gotten away from her then, I would have, too.

"My father didn't ask for custody of me; I think my mother's giving up killed his spirit. He didn't know how to live without her. He just … floated away.

"Shortly after, Papi fell sick. It soon became clear that he didn't have much time. He called me to him and told me that he was going to make right the mistake he made with *mi madre*. He made me sit and listen, and he told me of this legend that had been passed down through generations of our *familia*. He believed that the destruction of my family was his punishment for not telling the legend to my mother when she was young. He hoped to make it right by telling me in my youth.

"I didn't want to listen. I never wanted anything to do with those old superstitions. But Papi insisted, and in the end, I gave in. He was a dying man, and that is a strong force.

"But his age had made him forgetful, and he could not recall the details of the legend.

"He told me of a man who was part-crow. He said the man had come to this world from another. The Land of the Dead? Papi kept saying *los muertos*, but I did not understand.

"The man had escaped from those who wanted to kill him—I don't know who. Papi called them *matones*. Thugs, or killers.

"The man had made a new life, here in our world, and had fallen in love. His love, Juanita, was one of our

221

ancestors; this is why we had been tasked with passing down the legend.

"My mother, hearing the story too late, Papi said, had fallen in hopeless love with the crow-man, who had died centuries before, and was wasting away of an unrequited yearning.

"He said this was why we needed to hear the story when we were young. When I asked why we had to hear the story at all, he said, 'Otra vez.' Again. Another time. I never understood.

"I sensed that much was missing from the story. Papi's memory was not what it once was, and he had long thought the story unimportant, so it was not surprising that he forgot the details.

"I wanted to ask my mother to tell me, but when I saw her so empty with Papi's passing—he was her last tie to her former life other than me, and she hardly knew who I was—I couldn't. That story—and the crows—had hurt us enough. It was time for forgetting.

"After Papi died, my mother spiraled down. She dated a series of *pendejos*, who she brought round to our apartment. When one of them moved in, I left.

"When I did, I swore that those crow-creatures would never be allowed anywhere near my home or anyone I loved ever again.

"Maybe you think I'm crazy to blame it on them. Maybe I am. But every time I see one, I think of the crow-man my mother gave up her life for, whether he was real or not. She saw him in her mind all the same, and it destroyed her."

Though she had a sorry-feel for Slate's mother, Fannilea could not ignore her other thoughts. "Slate …" she whispered. There had been another. One like her! And he had escaped the Murder and lived his life as human. Maybe. "This crow-man. He could be the key. If he escaped the Murder … however he did it, it could help me. I could be rid of them. Forever."

Maybe even without the kekking contract, she thought.

Her hands wild-trembled; there was no controlling it. "We must go to see your mother."

She pushed off the bench and paced a strip of roof, consumed by sizzle-sparks.

"My mother," Slate said, his voice-tone flat.

"Please. Try to understand. This matters, big, to my whole life."

The iron had returned.

"*Cabrona* crow. Stubbornest bastards ever."

With great care and honey-slow movement, Fannilea got down on her knees in front of him. He waved his hands to stop her, but she stayed down and looked him in the eye. "What do you want? For taking me. I will do anything. I have to know about this man. I have to hear your mother's story."

"Stop," he said, sharplike. "Don't do that. We'll trade. As equals."

He waited for her to stand up.

When she did, he said, "I still want you to leave the house."

Fann closed her eyes against the hurt. "Of course," she said. "I will go immediately after. But ... is this because you now know I am crow?"

"No. It's because you lied to us."

After that, Slate did not say anything for a long time.

Fann sat next to him on the bench, not close enough to touch, watching the rising sun set the sky aflame, letting the gray-eyed boy fight his own demons, not interrupting, but living there with him for one or two human-minutes.

Finally, when the sun had risen to a shining yellow ball above, Slate asked, "You mean to escape them?"

"I have already disavowed them."

"Then let's go see *mi mamá*."

Chapter Twenty-Eight

Slate's mother lived in a small row house in Queens with white siding and a dark red roof. A chain-link fence surrounded a tiny square patch of yard.

At the corner of the lawn, a rose bush grew. Its branches sprangled through the fence as though it yearned to escape. The bush should have been nothing but bare twigs at this time of year, but at the top, climbing high, a lone rose bloomed, defying the odds.

Comforted Fann, it did.

Slate had not said a word to her on the train. She had let the silence be. What was there to say when you were on the verge of parting? Words seemed to mean more—and yet also much less.

At the gate, Slate stopped, one hand on the fence. "She didn't used to be like this," he said.

"I know."

"Before, she was the most beautiful woman in my world."

"I will remember that," Fann whisper-said. "Thank you for bringing me."

There was a wrong-feel moment of no words, and then Slate nodded and said, "*Sí*," with a quicklike voice-tone, not dwelling. He kept his head down and turned to lead her along the path to the house.

Were his shoulders low? She wanted to touch him but didn't dare.

What she felt didn't have to be returned. His iron-strength and self-pride made her feel safe with him, even if he had cast her out. He stayed with what he thought was right and true, and he had smart reasons for it, and that was a good-feel for her. It was not like shek, and for that she was grateful.

He opened the door and showed her through. She smiled shylike from under her lashes. Did his shoulders get more straight or did she think-dream it? She wasn't sure.

Inside, he called down the front hallway. "Mamá?"

There was no reply. He gestured for Fann to follow him.

The small kitchen had worn vinyl flooring. A brown table covered in chinks and dents filled the eat-in space, surrounded by matching chairs. One of the chairs balanced crookedly against the table; missing a leg, it was.

Slate's mother sat in one of the other chairs, sloped low over the table. The rich, spicy scent of cloves filled the room, and a cloud of smoke rose from an ashtray. At her fingertips stood a lowball glass half full of honey-colored liquid. Her hair lay thick with grease.

"Mamá?"

"What do you want?" Her voice-tone crunched like wheels on gravel. "Now you come to see me? After sending me away? Saying you don't want to know me?"

"Fann wants to ask you some questions. It's important." Fann watched him try and fail to stop himself from wincing as he said the next part. "About *el cuervo-hombre.*"

His mother cackled. "I told you they would not leave you be. Run all you like, but they're everywhere! They destroyed Azeel. They will destroy us, too." Her hands shook as she took a long drag on the cigarette.

"Azeel? Was that his name?" Fann stepped into the kitchen, delicatelike, not wanting to upset the strange balance here.

Slate's mother turned on her with dark half-lidded eyes. "Why you so interested in crow-people, *brujita*? *Son peligrosos.*"

"*Mamá. Esta bien. Tranquila.* She knows. Tell us Azeel's story, *por favor.*"

"*¿Y por que?* It's only trouble. Didn't your papi tell you?"

"Papi couldn't remember most of it. The details are important to Fann."

"Details, hmm? Why's that?" She peered at Fannilea, marking her features one by one with her eyes. "You're not dark like them. But it's hard to say, with those *cuervos*. Maybe you have a disguise? You are one of them, is that it?"

"I don't think she means to harm us, Mamá. At least, I don't think it can hurt to tell the story."

"*Sí,*" his mother said. "*Por favor, sientate.*" She gestured at the functional chairs.

When they were seated, she turned her gaze on Slate. "First tell me when you're coming home, *mijo*."

"I told you when I left. Get rid of Julio. Stop smoking. Don't drink so much. And forget about the crow-man. If you won't, then I make my own way."

Fannilea's heart ached. Slate's mother had hurt his life. So he had left. But maybe it was not all her fault. Not like the Murder. Perhaps it was the Murder that had made her this way, as Slate had said.

"Please, *señora*," Fann said.

"Call me Carla, *querida*. I am not so old yet for that *señora* stuff. So you want to know about *mi cuervo-hombre*, eh?"

Fann clutched the edge of the table with white knuckles. "I would like to know if the crow-man—Azeel—escaped the *matones*."

"Ach, *matones*. Papi was a mess at the end. He had forgotten most of the story long ago on purpose. I should have been the one to tell you, Rafa."

Slate rolled his eyes. "It's for her."

"Still not listening ...? Well, how can I blame you, after what it's done." She took a swig from the glass, licked her lips, and said, "Azeel, *mi amor*, where shall we start? I guess it will be where it always starts, nah? With the shadow of death. The land of *los muertos*.

"This is the story of Azeel, *el cuervo-hombre*, as *mi abuela* Sofia told it to me, as her mother told it to her, and her mother before that, so long back that no one remembers who told it first."

Carla paused. Then she took a deep breath and began.

CHAPTER TWENTY-NINE

"Deep in the uncanny realms, there is a dark place where human souls keep until the end of time. This place is known as the Otherworld. When the body passes, the spirit must make its way to this place. But sometimes spirits get lost. Sometimes they are pulled back or tied down by past lives, unable to move on. Thus, a secret race of guides evolved, meant to ferry the souls from this world to the next.

These shape-shifters, half-human, half-crow, are known as the Kaa. The Kaa roost on the border of the Otherworld, and when they are called, they travel to the human world to fetch the poor lost souls. They live together as a communal group—a Murder—and they follow a strict code of conduct they call shek. One is like the other, and all obey shek. They lived in harmony and followed shek for an uncounted time— until there was Azeel.

"The crows of the Murder were all born dark-feathered, but Azeel's feathers shone a glassy ebony that ate up all the light. Despite this, Azeel's self-being brought lightness wherever he went, to his fellow Murder members and to the dead souls alike. He performed his duties right-well, winning the trust of the souls with little effort. But his Murder-family yet feared him, thinking his unusual color an ill omen.

Azeel did not feel the same as his crow-brethren, nor did he find the gray world of the Ahk comforting as they did. He found himself wishing to spend more time in the human world. At first, he told himself it was not shek, and he ought not think it. But as time went on, he could not ignore it. He was not happy, and he wanted to be. So he flew to the human world, found a place to call home, and hid from the Murder."

"For how long?" Fann asked. "How long did he stay? Did he bring anything with him?" Corley had said they could not survive without makeberries. Had Azeel found a way to do it?

"Patience, child. It is in the story. You must let it unfold as it will." Carla took a sip of the amber liquid before beginning again. "In the human world, Azeel fell ill. He did not know what was wrong with him— he could hardly stand. The Kaa rarely become ill, not being susceptible to human diseases, and so he found it strange.

"The next morning, he discovered on his doorstep a large pouch full of the food of his people, makeberries of the Ahk. He gobbled up a handful and instantly began to feel better."

Fann's heart sank. Then it was true: She needed the makeberries. There would be no escaping the Murder without their consent. But who left the pouch on Azeel's doorstep? Who had helped him?

"Thus Azeel knew he needed makeberries to survive, but still he refused to return to the Ahk. He kept the rest of the makeberries cool to preserve them, and every day after that he ate a few. When the pouch held no more, he went to bed, uncertain what to do. But the next morning, just when he needed them, another large pouch arrived on his doorstep. Azeel did not see who delivered them.

"After some time living this way in the human world, Azeel met a soft-spoken brown-skinned woman who found his humor-lit black eyes and smooth black hair and careful way of looking at her enchanting, and they fell in love. Knowing the Murder as he did, Azeel feared their interference. He thought it best to try to stop it before it started.

"And so, for the first time, Azeel returned to the Murder. He told his crow-family of his desire to live as human, in a way of his own making. He asked their forgiveness for escaping. He requested that they release him from the Murder."

Fannilea gripped the edge of the table with scared, white fingers. Wasn't it as she had spoken to the

Murder, too? She feared she already knew how this story would end.

"Azeel did not mention the woman he loved, Juanita, whom he had already wed in the human way. He feared what the Murder would say or do about it.

"His requests fell on deaf ears. The Murder said that he, of all Kaa, with his gifted touch, had a duty to the lost souls. That he must use his talent to help them. They insisted that he was a member of the Murder, for then and for always—he belonged to them.

"But Azeel did not give up easily. He begged. He pled. He spoke passionately. He talked of the wonderful things in the human world. Over and over, he asked why. Why was he bound to a role he had not chosen, that he did not want, when so many others took it on with delight? Why must he bow to the Murder when he had different wishes for himself?

"Always the response was the same.

"'You belong to us.'

"'It is shek.'

"Still Azeel did not lose hope. He was sure that if he said the right words, they would understand.

"But there was only one thing left that he'd held back. Surely it would be the thing to convince them. And so, despite his fears, Azeel told the Murder about his love, Juanita.

"He told them about Juanita's warm brown eyes and long brown hair, about her small nose and large mouth, about the way the sun smelled against her skin and the way his heart leapt with joy when she laughed. He told them how she always knew when he'd need a cup of tea and made it just the way he liked. He told them how she never liked tight clothing; instead she wore loose and flowing dresses and skirts. He told them how much she loved to be barefoot and about the way she would sink into sand and squish it between her toes.

"Azeel fell into a sort of trance; he pictured Juanita and described what he saw, hoping that his fellow Murder members would feel what he felt through his words. He remembered every last detail of his love, and he told it all to that Murder of crows who did not want him to have her, in a desperate final attempt to make them understand.

"After the passing of much time, Azeel ran out of things to say. If there was more to Juanita than what he'd said, he did not know it.

"But the Murder told him nothing.

"When they let him return to the human world, he thought he had done it. He had convinced them.

"He went back to his life with Juanita, and the two were happy. Azeel accepted a position as a professor at a local college. He and Juanita bought a small house. Azeel did not think of the Murder.

"Until one day when he came home from teaching, he found the front door of his small house standing open. Filled with eerie dread, he wandered through the still, silent house to the bedroom.

"There she lay, on the bed they shared, her dark hair spread around her on the pillows. There was not a mark on her, and there was not a drop of spilled blood, but Azeel knew that she was gone. The spark he had known, the flame that had drawn him to her, had been extinguished. She was not his Juanita any longer.

"A great emptiness seized Azeel. He knew it would never leave him, but he also knew that he must not let it suck away the other emotion that rushed in: anger. He would hold his anger, and he would use it.

"He did not cry. He went to the kitchen and fetched the shears. Back in the bedroom, he cut a lock of Juanita's lovely long brown hair and laid it on the nightstand.

"He stepped back and changed to crow. Sweeping the curl up into his claws, he flew to the Ahk, feeling the emptiness wanting to grow inside him. He fanned the anger to keep the ache at bay.

"When he arrived, he found the Murder celebrating.

"'Our dear Azeel!' they greeted him. 'You've come home!'

"He wanted to kill them all.

"At the top of the tree perched a raven. Larger than the Murder-crows, it oversaw the proceedings with a watchful gaze. It peered at him with keen eyes. Azeel had not had occasion to meet her before, but he knew this must be the goddess of War and Death—the Morrigan. He did not know why she was there, but he was not afraid of her. If she supported what the Murder had done, then she was as evil as they.

"He showed them the lock of Juanita's hair. 'The hair of my love,' he said. 'Who you have taken from me.'

"'We are your love,' they said. 'We are your only love.'

"'You are nothing to me. I am leaving, and I am never coming back. If you want to make me, you will have to kill me.'

"The Murder blinked at him.

"The Morrigan swooped. She cawed and attacked. Her beak plucked at his breast feathers, sharp and hard. She scrabbled at his wings, searching for purchase with her claws.

"Her beak jabbed into his shoulder.

"The Murder hekked with delight.

"Azeel snapped out of his shock. He flapped at her, upsetting her balance. He pecked back, and he aimed for the eyes.

"She dodged, but her claws slipped on the pebbles, and she lost her footing. Azeel pounced.

"On top, he used his weight, though it was less than hers, to keep her pinned. This was easier than he might have thought it would be.

"Digging his beak deep into her feathers, he closed on one and yanked with all his might. It ripped free of the Morrigan's wing, and he brandished it aloft.

"The Murder fell silent.

"Azeel had won a battle with the goddess—this was no small thing.

"Carefully Azeel set the feather on the ground. Holding it with one claw, he used his beak to wrap the lock of Juanita's hair tight around it. Once he was sure the hair would not come loose, he dragged the feather to the base of the tree.

"Overripe makeberries collected there and rotted, fermenting. Azeel dragged the crow feather through one of the piles.

"The Morrigan's raven eyes glinted.

"She had not made a sound when he pulled her feather—and she did not make a sound now, only watched him with her wise eyes.

"The makeberry juice hardened on the feather and the hair, fusing them into a single unbreakable piece.

"'Whoever bears this talisman in future is under my protection!' Azeel announced. He did not know if this would work—he could only hope that the Morrigan would honor the results of the battle she'd lost.

"He swept the talisman in his beak and flew to the top of the tree. There he yanked off a thin branch drooping with makeberries. Without a backward glance or a cawed goodbye, he left the Ahk behind.

"He wasted no time on his return flight. In a short while he arrived at his small house, the site of so much happiness, now a place of darkness.

"That night, he sat with Juanita through the dark hours. He did not think of the Murder. Only of her.

"In the morning, as the sun turned their bedroom a warm yellow, Azeel ate the makeberries he'd brought from the Ahk one by one. Would they be the last he consumed?

"Then he kissed his beloved for the last time, the taste of makeberry juice still on his tongue.

"As he eased away, she sighed. Azeel froze, listening, watching. Did she yet live? Had he imagined it? He could not tell.

"He sat with her longer, waiting and watching, but she made no further sound nor movement. And thus

Azeel's love was gone from him, destroyed by the Murder.

"It is not known what happened to him after that. Without makeberries, how could he survive? Some say he found a way to live without. Did the Murder come after him yet again? No one knows. Some say he wanders the world to this day."

Carla stopped speaking. She took another drag on the cigarette and raised her eyebrows at them.

"That's it. That's the story of my crow-man. Romantic, nah?"

Fann's eyes widened. Romantic? No. Torture. The same torture she knew.

"I see how you look, *querida*, but I mean his love for Juanita. So pure and true, no? After hearing of it, I could not think my own love measured up. It seemed pale. Although now . . ."

Her eyes darted toward Slate's face, but did not quite make it there.

"Well. It has been a long time."

She took a last long drag and then stubbed the cigarette out.

"But ..." Fann said. "Who brought him the makeberries? Who helped him? He had some here. Did he try to plant them, so he could survive? How can no one know what happened to him after he returned? What about the Murder—did the Murder leave him alone?" How could there be such a story, and yet no answers in it? Fann clenched a fist with frustration.

"Azeel never knew who brought the berries. Or if he did, he didn't include it in the story. If he tried to plant the berries, I'm sure they would have died. Things of *los muertos* never survive in the world of the living. I'm sure if there were good answers to your questions, Azeel would have included them in his story."

"Why do you say that?"

"Because that's why he told the story. That's why he insisted *we* tell the story. In case there was another, like him. An escapee ... from her people." Her eyes slit-slatted, directed at Fann.

"*Otra vez,*" Slate whispered. "That's what Papi meant."

"Right," Fann said, trying to hide her nerve-shake. "Just in case. But how could he know? That ... the other one would hear the story? That ... the other one would find one of you?"

"That is a question *the other one* would be better able to answer than I," Carla said. "Perhaps she might think about how she came to know me. Or my son."

But Fann did not have a chance to consider this before Carla continued.

"Telling this story has reminded me of something, *mijo*. I found it in your grandfather's things after he died. I was going to throw out his old papers when I noticed something he meant to give you."

Slate scowled. "He tried. I don't want it."

"You must take it. Especially now."

Carla pushed back from the table and stood with some difficulty, then hobbled out of the room.

"What is she talking about?" Fann asked.

Slate didn't answer her.

Clara returned with her right hand balled in a fist. She opened it over the table and slid something toward Slate. He made no move to catch it.

Fann put her hand up just in time. The object bounced against her palm. It had been strung on a piece of thin black cord, like a necklace, but she could hardly believe what she was looking at. It was a hardened chunk of makeberry juice. Frozen inside, a single shiny black raven feather wrapped in dark brown human hair hung suspended.

Fann's crow-heart skipped a beat. She couldn't make her mouth work.

"The bearer of the story is to bear the pendant," Clara said. "To wear it, for protection. Should the Murder come seeking its own."

Her dark eyes burned into Fann's lighter ones.

"I don't want it." Slate wouldn't look at it.

"Doesn't matter. It's yours."

"Thank you," Fann said, quietlike. The talisman felt warm in her palm. "For telling us the story. And for the … this. It is no light thing, for me."

"*De nada*, young one. If you are a crow, then perhaps you are less like the Kaa and more like Azeel."

Fann clutched the pendant tense in her fist. Dared she hope? Azeel had lost his love, true. But he had escaped. He had won his freedom. Maybe. Perhaps. Might-be.

And now she held the small symbol he had left behind.

Otra vez.

CHAPTER THIRTY

Fann was the sort to keep her promises. She would leave Shady House, but there were three small things she had to do first.

One, she searched the kitchen. There she found a medium-sized glass jar with a tight-fitting lid. She dumped her new stash of makeberries into it and sealed the lid as tight as it would go. Wok, grew small in the jar, they did.

She counted. Fifteen. Three a day, Corley had said. That was only five days. One day shy of her end-of-contract. Not good. But nothing she could do now. She added the jar to the bag Leaf had packed for her, stuffing it into the middle of a blanket for safe-keep.

Two, she went down to the basement. There she found a small orange pot and a bag of soil. They wouldn't fit in her bag, so she tossed the soil-bag into the pot and decided to carry them.

One more thing, then, and she would have to go. Wetness crept behind her eyes, and she poked at them.

It wasn't the place. Any place could become home, with the right things-done. But ... the people. Those were different.

Hadn't known them long, had she? Only a week. But sometimes it went that way, she guessed. Sometimes you met someone and that was it; they were in your heart. What could you do?

She would keep them there and hope for the best.

Bag slung over her shoulder, pot with soil cradled in her arms, Fann bumped against Slate's half-open bedroom door instead of knocking.

"It's late," he said. "You don't have to leave this second. Stay the night, if you want."

"It's all right," she said, ignoring his up-and-down voice-tone. She could not go back and forth now, or she would not keep her promise. "I'm ready. There's … one more thing."

She set the pot down and dug into her pocket. Then she held her hand out. In the center of her palm was the feather pendant.

"I don't want that."

"You must keep it."

"I won't take it."

"It might protect you. I … want you to wear it. Please."

"You won't know if I do or not. You won't be here."

More of that up-and-down voice-tone. It made her want to lay her crow-heart before him, so he could see what was inside. But her people had ruined this, too. They had damaged him too much already. She must wait and hope for a better moment. This was not the time, for that, for him.

"Wear it. If they come for you …"

The things she wanted to say, they were many. The Murder would follow her, she hoped, and leave the house alone. If they didn't, she would stop them.

Somehow.

"Here," she said, dropping the pendant on the desk. "I'll trust you."

"Misguided," Slate said.

"Maybe," Fann said. "But I'll never know for sure, will I? And so I can trust as I like."

Fann picked up her pot and turned for the door, listening. But, like before, he did not stop her, and so she walked, one step at a time, in the silence, without looking back, for she knew that if she looked back she might not make it to the door. She kept walking, not looking, down the stairs and down the hall and out the front door—and into the wideness of the whole human world, on her own, leaving behind the boy of iron she yearned to know.

Chapter Thirty-One

The left-empty house she'd slept in before felt even more left and empty. Last time, she had been alone and wanting, liking, needing it that way. This time ...

But there was no time to dwell. She had to think of surviving.

There were six days left on her contract.

First, just in case, there was one thing she must do. In case the story couldn't be trusted, and knowing the

Murder, no stories where they were concerned should be trusted.

Carefullike, she set the orange pot on the floor and dumped the bag of soil into it. Using two fingers, she scooped out a tunnel in the middle. She took one berry from her stash and set it gentlelike at the bottom of the tunnel, then covered it. She sprinkled a dash of water over it, too, and that was done.

Beyond this, what could she do? She would not be able to tell the house members now. She had lost their trust.

Yet she could not give up.

Six days.

Late, it was, as Slate had said. Sleep, she must. At day-rising she would think better. See the options. If there were any.

But sleep had left her, too. She lay open-eyed, unquiet, her thoughts attacking her like angry crows, pecking her eyes and head and flapping at her face until she flinched and rose, before day-rising.

She left with nothing, to walk the world. The snow had gone, quicklike, and the ground lay stiff and frozen, not-friendly. The air-cold in her lungs struck like daggers, but made her move lively. The light hung gray for now, but the sun would shatter it soon. That, at least, she could count on.

What if she could see no way to win her contract? Then in six days, she must go to her rest.

Until that time, she would be here. And be here true, she would.

A rest lay over the city. The life of the place kept on, but there was less fastness now, less hurry-scurry. Four Chihuahuas pulled a woman on a leash, and one yapped at Fann, but she moved in a hushed cocoon, liking her space here. She felt the human world flow around her, move this way, change that way. It would go on when she didn't. Comfort there was, in that.

She passed a food-place with gleaming edges. Shiny silver could not be wrong.

She went inside.

"Do you have french fries?"

They did.

The order-taker held up his pen, waiting. "What else?"

"There is no more," Fann said.

He looked down his face at her, not approving, but she didn't mind.

When the fries came, she ate them one at a time, slow-chewing. Warm and rich and so-right, they were.

The order-taker gave her a snivelly nose as he passed, but she returned him a lopsided grin and snarfed another fry.

After breakfast, she rode the train.

People, all kinds, she saw. Looking like anything. From everywhere and also nowhere, ending up here, mixed up together.

A crow-girl was not so strange, here. She could belong. Or not, and that was fine, too. The city was hers, but she was not its. She liked it that way.

As she rode, she paid attention.

Just in case this was it. Just in case she could not fix it (she *would*, but just in case) and these six days were all she would get, of anything, ever again.

She noticed it all.

Even the not-right things—the smell of something sick-sweet from the skin of the passed-out man across the aisle, the metal-bark of some harsh sound from headphones over there, the air-clog-feel until the doors moved wide and let in the dagger-sharp air—came at her large and unruly and distinct. She let them hit her, feeling the whole city.

Humans, they did this, she knew. Moment-feeling. Some of them, a lot, like the only thing.

But she thought of what Scrap had said. About your thing-of-meaning. If she had it, to keep, this world with more days, she'd need that thing. Something bigger than moments.

Something to make, big and raw and deep of her. Something built with many day-risings and night-settings and with her whole soul. Something that made her go. Something true, that was hers.

When she had the long life, she would find that something.

If.

If she had the long life.

She got off the train. To the north, she saw the big park. She had not meant to come here, but her crow-self still lived within.

Her human heart urged her south, away; she did not want to let the crow out. But it was part of her, too, and wanting a fly of sorts. She faced the park and barreled up the path. The gnarly-branched trees waved her on. She followed her crow-heart, let it pull her into the brown and gray depths.

She wouldn't change, but—

She charged up a rock—and at the top, she discovered that she'd been flapping her arms. Not minding, she zoomed across the rock, still flapping. Back and forth over that rock, Fann flew and flew—at least, as close as she could get, there in the park, with arms for wings.

For the first time in her life, she did not feel that as not-right. She missed flying, she did, but other things mattered more.

Fann whirled and flapped without a way to go. She threw herself one way and the next, toward a stand of trees—stopped short.

There, above her, in the closest treetop, perched a roost of crows. A big black cloud, fallen from the sky like burnt-up lava or risen from the ground like floating ash, they were unfamiliar—no Kaa, and not the roost from Shady House. Know her, they wouldn't.

As she came near, one of the crows at the top *aw-aw-aw*ed wild and brittlelike. His voice-tone warned. The others joined him. They screeched and scolded.

They thought Fannilea Ishika Fiachra was a predator.

They thought she was *human*.

She cackled first. Then she whooped.

She cawed at the crows, a just-right echo. *Aw-aw-aw.* She flapped as she had before, with more joy now, knowing that the poor few humans near would think her mad, but not caring, for a small thought, an idea, bloomed at the back of her mind.

The crows blinked, not-sure.

Predator?

Or crow-friend?

She squawked at them, and laughed, and danced, and cried fat relief-tears, and as her glee grew and her human-heart swelled, the crows decided.

With one last flap of Fann's arms—not wings—the roost gathered and took flight, cawing and air-bursting, shouting to each other to beware the human.

Fann watched as they filled the sky, delighted by their yells. For the first time since Slate had seen his mother at the door, she felt hopeful, and she let that hope sing in both her hearts as the roost faded to specks on the horizon, for those silly old crows had done something good for once—they had made her think what she would do, and it might even work.

CHAPTER THIRTY-TWO

On the evening of the day after Christmas, a certain half-finished red brick house with a charming rooftop garden glowed softly, lit from within by white-gold fairy lights, a beacon below gray afternoon clouds that had settled over the city. Silver garlands decorated windows and doors, while glittering snowflakes twirled lazily, hanging on every stray nail. Inside, gypsy guitar music wafted from speakers. The clink and crash of dishes—and occasional laughter—sounded from the kitchen.

At first, no one noticed the intelligent blue eyes that peeped over the bottom pane of the dining room window. If anyone had, he might've expected to find sleek black feathers lining the bird skull that held those crow-sharp eyes, but this crow's feathers were a downy white.

Jayda set a stack of mismatched plates on the counter. "I miss Leaf. It's weird without her."

Moonbeam tossed a hard glance at Slate. "I miss Fann. It's not weird enough without her."

"Stop it," Slate said. "Leaf will be home soon."

Something caught his eye, over by the window. The flick of a feather? There. Low. Down by the sill. He peered, trying to see.

"What happened?" Scrap asked, following the direction of his gaze. "Holy … what is that? Is that a *crow*?"

"I thought crows were black," Moonbeam said.

"Does it have … blue eyes?" Jayda asked.

"It's an albino," Scrap said. "Weird."

"Is it watching us?" Moonbeam crept forward, one lithe step at a time, not wanting to scare the bird.

But the white crow didn't move a muscle. It watched, and it waited for the moonlight-haired girl to make her way over to it.

Moonbeam sidled up to the window and bent to look right into the bird's eyes.

It still didn't move.

"Does it seem familiar?" Moonbeam asked, tilting her head.

The crow tilted its head.

"Moonbeam," Slate said, a warning in his voice. "Don't."

The white crow opened its beak.

"Wok," it said.

"Yep," the blond girl said under her breath, low enough that Slate wouldn't hear. "You definitely remind me of someone."

She marched back to the kitchen.

"Moonbeam," Slate said. "Leave it be."

"I'm tired of your stupid rules!"

"Leave the house then," Slate said.

"Guys . . ." Jayda said, beseeching.

"Maybe I will!" Moonbeam shouted over her shoulder. "Leaf and Fann and I will leave and start our own house."

"She lied to you as much as to the rest of us."

"Maybe she had a good reason. Did you ever think of that?"

"The house rule is not 'be honest unless you have a good reason not to.'"

"What if somebody's life was in danger? What if telling could get someone killed? You don't know!"

"You're reaching. Anything to give her room."

"Somebody has to. You aren't giving her any."

"No liars allowed. You knew that when you joined the house."

Moonbeam glared at him, arms crossed over her chest.

"I'm feeding it," she said. "I don't care."

She threw open the refrigerator door and yanked out a crumpled paper bag. Cradling it against her, she marched to the door and pushed through it.

The white crow flew to meet her.

"She's feeding it french fries," Scrap said, shaking his head.

"Crows love french fries," Slate said. "*All* crows."

The white crow gobbled up the fries Moonbeam fed it, and nothing much more happened that evening between the crow and the humans of Shady House. But long after the french fries were eaten and Moonbeam had gone back inside, the white crow could be seen sitting on the windowsill. For as long as the house members ate their dinner and listened to their music and talked to each other in the dining room, the crow sat on the windowsill, watching from the outside. Even after the house members had gone to their beds, the crow remained.

Late in the night, as the house slept, one among the house members snuck down the stairs.

The crow still crouched on the sill, its head curled into its breast, its eyes closed.

The boy tapped on the window and the crow poked its head up.

"If you are who I think you are, you are breaking an agreement."

Blue crow-eyes met gray human ones. Both sets were steady. Both sets were sad.

They remained locked together for a long moment. Then the crow gave a painful cry, turned its back on the boy, and tore off into the night sky.

CHAPTER THIRTY-THREE

There are whispers. Isn't that how it often starts? Whispers. But this time ...

The whispers are a special kind of delicatelike. Much care. Much quiet.

The hints ... well.

We will not say the Morrigan has failed. Not-right, no-how, no-way. Not.

Our goddess, our heart. No-fail.

It is only … a right-moment. A right-moment for us, a thing we can do, that maybe the Morrigan has not seen. She has a schedule-full, being a goddess, of course she does.

Of course, sometimes right-moments, at the time, do not seem to make-right with shek. Sometimes … sometimes *stretching* is needed. Of course not a we-like-to-do. But if it would make our Murder whole—if it will bring that white-crow bitch—no, our confused crow-daughter!—home, well, then, yes. We will.

But does our awoah agree?

We bristle with waiting.

Datchett takes his perch and calls us to order. His glare halt-stops the last chitter-chatter, but brittle mind-feelings of a raw rumpus have stirred our blood. All beaks turn to be led, hoping for a call to arms. Something must be done!

Datchett wide-spreads his wings, embrace-showing. He flaps us closer, and we gather, harsh-breathing.

"You, my crow-children, know what's happening, so I won't say mind-tricks to you. You are too sharp for that. Things have risen up with our crow-daughter; she has shown her true-self to more humans. It is not good. Not good one bit."

We surprise-breathe, though all have known.

Datchett eyeballs Corley. The young crow's head droops, silentlike, and he won't look up to meet his awoah's gaze. Datchett lets him be, for the eye-blink.

"We have a rare chance now. You know of what I speak. You know what it will need." Datchett pauses to allow his words to sink in. "It will not be easy. There will be fighting back. If we are to make-right, we will need the full-heart joining in of *every* member. If there are any who are not heart-able of this, please speak."

Datchett tilts his head in the direction of Manak and Corley, who perch on the same branch, huddled together, one hair apart.

Neither of them speaks nor looks.

Of course taking action against one's nestling or nestling-mate is not easy, but if it is best for the Murder, none should be so low-ugly as to put one life before the many. It would not be shek-right.

"Then," Datchett said. "There is one last thing. A pretend-fuss will be needed. Of course, it will be best if those who make it are those she is least like to be suspecting, wok?"

Datchett eyeballs us, blanklike, but we know his meaning. Head of feathers after head of feathers turns; pair upon pair of beady-sharp eyes dagger into two just-right Murder members—Manak Deshai and Corley Drust Fiachra.

Under the eye-storm, Corley shiver-shakes. He judders so hard the branch rattles, but he keeps his head down and holds tight. When the strange pulses die, leaving his feathers askew, Corley raises his head.

"I will do it."

"Corley," Manak hisses, "she is your nestling-mate; you're not bound—"

In the bitty-fine detail, it is sharp-rightly true that Murder members are not bound to act against nestling-mates. But one sometimes found the bitty-fine detail and the true-world needs of shek to be not exactly in one line.

"I will do it," Corley repeats, ignoring Manak.

Manak fluffs his feathers, unsettledlike. He does not like it. But he cannot let his last-alone nestling take on such a danger-filled mission by himself. The white-feathered girl will have help. Corley ought, as well.

"I will go with him," Manak says.

"Excellent!" Datchett hops joyful. "I am well pleased. I believe that settles everything, dear Murder. Make yourselves ready for riik. We leave at day-rising in the human world."

CHAPTER THIRTY-FOUR

Fannilea Ishika Fiachra hated hospitals. Hard, empty places. The ugly-sweet scent of death on top of everything. The glaring lights and the echoing halls. Of course, they also put her in mind of that riik. The Boneman. What the Murder had done, or not done. She had hoped not to set foot in another. But she had to see Leaf. Was she breathing? Living still? Fann needed to know with her own eyes.

Nerve-tingles skitter-scattered along her skin. She watched, her neck moving, quicklike, crowlike— forgetting that she could move her eyes without her head. A wrong-footed step, and her shoes squawked. She flinched. She did not want to run into the iron-boy. Or the other house members. Or Leaf's mother.

She tracked the room numbers ... 280 ... 282 ... 284. Leaf's room. She listened. No sound from inside. Taking a deep breath, she peered around the corner.

Leaf lay in the bed. A tiny birdlike thing, she was, hooked up to a bag by plastic veins. Her skin hung blue and flat; her sunken cheeks were razor-sharp. Black half-moons bloomed beneath her eyelids.

Fann wanted to gather her up and beg her to wake. Instead, she slumped into one of the chairs, afraid to touch the pale girl.

A handful of sunflowers smiled from a vase on the drawer-chest, bringing a bloom of yellow to the deathly room.

Jayda. Jayda would bring those.

Fann clutched at the arms of the chair. How she missed Jayda. Already!

"What am I going to do?" she moaned.

Her brilliant plan to hang around the house as a crow had not helped. Plus, she *had* promised Slate, even if there hadn't been anything in the promise about crow or human. If only she could talk to Leaf. The chickie-lion girl would have twenty billion ideas Fann hadn't thought of.

"Leaf, I . . ."

So still, so quiet, so almost-broken.

But she was all Fann had.

The words began to spill, rumble-tumble at first, and then with more sense. Fann told Leaf all the bits she'd missed. About looking for her with Slate. What it was like to walk with him, the strange and deep and yet easy feeling of it. Finding the crow feather. Accusing the Murder. The way Slate had looked at her when she'd returned, like he was looking at the wall.

"He hates me, Leaf," she said. "But how can I explain? How can I tell them? If the Murder would hurt you, they'll hurt them. It's better for them to hate me than to get hurt and end up ... like this. It's better for me to stay away, as he asked."

Fann scooched the chair forward, closer to the bed. Leaf's hand lay inches from her own.

"But ... there's more. I didn't want to tell them because I didn't think they could accept it. But ..."

She remembered the moon girl's face, large above her, shining with delight as the white crow in her hand pecked at the french fries she'd offered.

"Moonbeam seems to know."

Fann traced the blue veins on the back of Leaf's pale hand with her eyes. She wished the girl would wake and speak, tell her something, so that she did not have to say the next part out loud on her own. But Leaf did not wake, and Fann could avoid it no longer.

"I wondered. What if it's not them who won't accept it? My whole life ... I was taught—no, *trained*—to never let any human know what I am. I had to hide. Not get too close. Not be too open. What if ... What if they trained me too well? What if I can't be open? Can't be myself?" She whispered, "What if I can't tell the truth? What if I can't accept myself and be true, with who I am, in the open? In the world, either one?" Fann reached for Leaf's hand. "I did with you, I know.

You made it easy. The others … it's not the same. I don't know if I can do it, with them. I …"

Something flickered at the corner of Fann's vision— near Leaf's face? But when she turned to focus, she saw no movement.

"Leaf?" Her heart pounded.

Had the girl's brow been creased like that before? Her mouth pursed? She couldn't remember.

Something pressed against Fann's fingers. Harder, squeezing. Leaf was squeezing her hand.

"Leaf? I'm here!"

Leaf let out a low moan.

"Wake up, please, I'm here."

The pressure on Fann's fingers ceased, and Leaf's face cleared.

Snappy-sharp and fight-ready, Fann sat on the edge of the chair, waiting, but Leaf did not move again.

She had, though. She had squeezed Fann's hand, just when Fann said she didn't know if she could tell the others. Even unconscious, Leaf knew what had to be done, one way or another.

It was time for Fann to find the courage to do it.

CHAPTER THIRTY-FIVE

How hard it was for Fann to change to crow and fly back to the house. But she was short on time and money, and there seemed no other way. It would be fastest. Rumbly clouds hung low over the city, and as she flapped, they started to drop mushy-fat snowflakes. Freezy water splatted on her head, and it put her in mind of the night Leaf had been hurt. She fast-fluttered her lashes to clear her eyes.

It hurt to fly. The cold metal in her crooked wing burned icy against her skin-insides. Or no … that wasn't right. She struggled to stay in the air. Hard work, it was, this flying thing. Maybe she should have walked.

Wok?

She snapped her beak. She must not lose hold now. This moment mattered too much. Everything, now, depended on how the house members reacted to what she was about to tell them.

It was as the Morrigan had decreed.

But as Fann flew, she couldn't help wondering, as had long been her wont—*why?* Why should her life be in the hands of others? Why should everything she wanted depend on what they thought of her? Why should she have to twist herself in knots to gain their approval in order to be free?

It didn't seem fair.

It didn't seem right or true.

The house appeared in her sight, and Fann whuffed with good-feeling. The change back was not long away. Had she liked it this much before? She didn't think.

She swooped into the backyard, her crow-heart beating hard.

In the kitchen, Moonbeam sat at the table, munching on rice crackers and flipping through an old magazine. A flash of white dropped past the window. When she glanced up, her gaze met the white crow's.

"Jayda! Scrap!"

When they came, Moonbeam pointed, words lost.

Scrap narrowed his eyes, thoughtful.

"The roost has moved on," Jayda said.

"I don't think this one is part of the roost," Moonbeam said. She marched to the door and flung it open.

"Want to come in?" she asked the crow, holding out her arm.

The white-feathered crow hopped forward, but stopped at the edge of the windowsill, its head cocked.

Glancing back at Jayda and Scrap, Moonbeam said, "The other one's not here. He went to the hospital."

The white-feathered crow bobbed its head and hopped onto Moonbeam's arm. The girl stepped back inside, carrying the bird delicately.

"This is weird," Scrap said. "Crows aren't supposed to be *that* used to people, are they?"

"Sometimes," Moonbeam said. "Sometimes people keep them as pets. But I think this one's special. I think she'll explain everything herself."

Jayda had backed up, away from the crow. "She?"

Moonbeam brought the crow into the kitchen, where she squatted and set her palm on the floor so that her arm formed a ramp.

"Check out her left wing."

The crow waddled down Moonbeam's arm and hopped away. Its left wing hung askew.

"That wing has been broken," Scrap said.

"Remind you of anyone?"

With the house members looking on, the crow's body began to tremble. A tremor in its left wing spread to the right and then down through its claws. The tiny jolts built to jarring shock waves, shaking the crow's whole body.

"Is it having a seizure?" Scrap asked. "What should we do?"

Moonbeam bit her lip. "Wait one second, I think."

The crow dropped its head, and the shudders held it, bursting through wings and claws and beak, until—

The crow exploded up and out in a flurry of feathers. Bird-shape lengthened, grew, and rounded out. Feathers turned to skin, claws to feet, wings to limbs, beak to nose and mouth, head feathers to a thatch of unkempt white hair. Beneath that hair, the same blue eyes that had watched them from the white crow's head now watched them from Fann's.

Scrap's mouth dropped open.

Moonbeam wore a small, self-satisfied smile.

Jayda's eyes shone glassy and distant. Fann could only hope she'd be able to turn the girl back to warm with her words.

"I have to say a lot, but first is that I'm sorry. I did not tell you what I should have. I … stuck my b—nose where I shouldn't. I broke the house rules, good rules. I thought I had to, and I will explain why, but I never liked it. It did not seem right. And so I am sorry for not learning it sooner."

"Yeah, Slate would've wanted to know you were a crow before he let you have a trial," Scrap said.

Fann couldn't tell from his voice-tone whether it was a joke or not.

"Crow, not exactly. Kaa, it is."

She told them of the Murder, their role as spirit guides, their life in the Ahk, and of shek, as she had both Leaf and Slate before.

"If you're one of them and you're supposed to live there, then what are you doing here?" Jayda asked, arms crossed.

"Is someone going to die?" Moonbeam asked, fascinated.

"No. Kaa come after someone is dead, and all at once, as a Murder. I am here ... I am here alone, because I have left them. I am here because I don't want to be Kaa. I want to be human."

"You want to leave the people you belong to. Forever." Jayda's voice-tone bit hard, spikelike.

"Shek ... shek is like chains. Worse. Because you can't see them and take them off and be free. You are bound, not by your choice but by the accident of your birth. You are here, alone, in Shady House. Where are *your* people?"

"Shady House is my people."

"The ones you chose. Because you could. But what about the ones you were born to? Where are they?"

Understanding flickered in Jayda's eyes, but the girl did not melt.

Fannilea told them the rest. About her early attempted escape, about the erawk, and finally, about the Boneman. About what it was like to recover from her meeting with the Boneman.

"My arm took many months to heal, and I will never be able to make it straight all the way again." She showed them. "But my wing ... I couldn't fly, at first. I taught myself, with much work. Much pain. Much fear. I would not give up. I learned to fly again."

"Slate was right. You weren't straight with us," Jayda said, arms still crossed.

"She had kind of a lot of reasons not to be," Moonbeam said, chewing on her hair. "I bet there's a rule. That she's not supposed to tell us."

"Yes. The existence of our race is to remain a secret."

"Then why tell us now?" Jayda addressed Moonbeam, but Fann answered her.

"Because I was wrong not to. I was wrong to follow their bad-for-life, forced-on-me rules and not the house's. You should know who you deal with. I want to be true. Not-hiding. That's what I always wanted to be. I'm sorry. If I could have chosen to have been born human, I would have. I would do it now; I would have done it as a nestling. But this is what I am, and I must do what I can to free myself of it."

Jayda's jaw shifted, one way, then the other. Her brown eyes had gone glossy.

"I accept your apology," Moonbeam said.

Fann bowed her head to her.

Moonbeam leaned in toward Jayda. "Regardless of where or what she was born, she isn't one of them. She's one of us. Leaf has known that all along."

Jayda stepped back, shaking her head. "I don't know. Slate was right. She lied. She broke the trust. This house works because we're honest with each other. Without that ..."

"But being honest doesn't mean sharing every single thought we have. It means not faking, right? It means not trying to get something by faking. I don't think

Fann did that. Do you?" Moonbeam turned to Scrap, who had moved closer. "Scrap?"

"You're here now," Scrap said softly to Fann. "If what you did before was a mistake, then your telling us now is enough for me."

Moonbeam wrangled him into a giant hug. "S'why I love you, Scrappy-chan!"

Over Moonbeam's arms, Scrap looked at Jayda. "Jay?"

Jayda shook her head, tightlike. "I don't—"

A clatter sounded at the dining room window, and all heads turned.

Two crows beat their wings at the glass, a big shiny black one and a smaller one with faint white stripes on his wings.

Once they had the house members' attention, they opened their beaks and sang.

The Het Ket Wok Aw Aw! Fannilea's crow-heart tumbled open. They had come for her!

Great joy bright-sparkled in her, though she could not tell why, and she ran to the back door to meet her crow-family.

CHAPTER THIRTY-SIX

On the back step of the red brick house, Fannilea welcomed her nest.

"Corley! Manak!" she crowed.

They were here! They were here! All was joy. All was right and true. The part of her that felt confused lay quiet, overshadowed.

Two black crows swirled and danced and changed, shifting from bird to human. Dressed in their shifts, they were, and all embraced together when the change was complete.

So strong was Fannilea's delight that she wanted to let water leak from her eyes at the seeing of them. Leap on them, game-play, allopreen their soft-feathered faces, she wanted, and yet ... something held her.

That confused part. Not-right, it was. Welcoming, she felt, to see them, that was all, or it should be all, and yet it wasn't. She had an ugly squish-place, inside. Something not true, with these two, her nestling-mate and her crow-uncle, who raised her from a peeping chick. But how could that be?

"We have clothes here," Corley said. "Help from local crows. Let us be more human and visit with you."

They retreated behind the pine. When they emerged, Corley wore the same silly outfit he'd worn when he'd first come to see her, that too-big poncho that made Fannilea want to laugh with delight. Manak's hair lay lank with grease, and his leftover jeans bore wrinkles and stains.

Seeing them there, so human, snapped something home in Fannilea. Or was it the ending of that kekking song? She didn't know, but she returned to herself. She wriggled her fingers and rolled her shoulders. Human, she was. Not crow. These two had done her dear one— and, as such, *her*—a great wrong. She rubbed her temples, trying to wear away the last of the fog the song had brought on.

"You shouldn't have come."

"But we've come to say we're sorry," Corley said.

"The Murder wants you back," Manak said.

"The Murder has always wanted me back," Fann said. "It's I who doesn't want the Murder."

"Let us in," Corley said. "We want to sort this out. We want to help you return."

"I am not going to return," Fann said firmly.

"Fann," Manak said. "We are sorry. Please let us come in to tell you. Just a chance to explain."

This stopped her. A chance. To explain. This was all they asked? Hadn't she asked for the same from the house members? Shouldn't a chance to repair always be taken? How could she deny them that, the two who had once been her family?

She opened the door.

"Fann?" Doubt showed in Moonbeam's eyes.

As the two crow-men stepped inside, Corley opened his mouth and resumed singing.

The song danced round Fannilea, twining and winding and embracing, holding. It hummed along her bones. It vibrated in her mind, asking her to do the right and true thing, calling to her, seeming to set the world right. It was a thing of beauty, calling her to the side of her people, where she belonged. It was in her ears and in her veins and then it was in her mouth.

She sang.

There had been something ... something biglike ... something she didn't remember. Most biglike thing, joining the family, it was. She must. How could she be here, in this wrong place?

She drifted toward her crow-uncle. Three voices rose as one, joined, battle-ready.

But the house members heard nothing harmonious. The notes pecked at their ears; to them the Het Ket Wok Aw Aw sounded nothing like a song. The crow-people kekked and rawked and barked. And their friend's eyes turned flat and distant and unseeing.

"Fann!" Moonbeam shouted. "Make them stop!"

Fann made no change.

"We have to stop them," Moonbeam said. "Now."

She raced across the room, leapt on Corley, and clamped a hand over his mouth. "Shut up, you nasty bird! Leave her be! She doesn't belong to you!"

As the song lost power, Fann faltered. What had she been thinking of?

Moonbeam looked around wildly for Scrap, but he had disappeared.

"Jayda," she screamed. "Jayda, help me!"

Jayda stood frozen, uncertain, across the room.

Corley thrashed, trying to dislodge Moonbeam's hand, but the willowy girl clung to him like a monkey, scrabbling against his back, determined to hold on. He spun and bucked.

"Jayda, please!"

Jayda turned and headed for the kitchen, leaving Moonbeam hanging from the crow-boy's back.

Manak eyed them from a safe distance and kept singing.

A loud bang sounded in the kitchen.

"Heads up!" Jayda yelled, and something the size of a tea saucer careened along the dining room floor and wobbled to a stop at the feet of a still-squirming Corley.

It was the roll of duct tape from the kitchen junk drawer.

Moonbeam's tongue poked out through her slow, wide grin.

Jayda stalked back into the dining room with steely-dark brown eyes trained on Manak. He dared to look at her, once, and she smiled with so much politeness that he cowered.

"I'm sorry, but I *really* don't like this song," she said.

With Jayda menacing the scrawny older crow-man, who sang in a frenzy now, faster and faster, struggling to keep Fann in thrall as he backed away from the tall, lithe girl, Moonbeam afforded herself a moment of assessing how far away that duct tape was. She thought she could scoop it up if she had a moment … if she could keep Corley from singing for just a second …

She kept her left hand on his mouth, and with the fingers of her right, she spidered up his face until she felt the give of his eye socket. Then she poked, hard.

Corley yelled, and Moonbeam let go.

Corley stumbled, covering his right eye, while Moonbeam leapt for the tape and yanked a piece off. She flung herself at the crow-boy again, using her body weight to send them both tumbling to the ground. Then she scrabbled up on her elbows and slapped the piece of tape over his mouth.

"Ha!" she shouted.

Corley reached up to try to rip it off, and she leapt onto his chest, straddling him and trapping his arms with her legs.

"I don't think so, crow-boy," she said sweetly. "You can just stay right where you are."

Manak, still trying to avoid Jayda, bumped into the door. He was trapped. As she stepped closer, he threw up his hands to protect his face.

"Don't hurt me," he whimpered.

With the silencing of the song, Fann frowned. "Wok?"

"Fann! Help me!" Moonbeam cried.

Corley thrashed wildly, trying to twist out from under Moonbeam.

Then Scrap spoke from the kitchen. "Let him go, Moonbeam."

"I can't let him go! He'll—whoa. Scrappy-chan, *what is that*?" She tumbled off Corley, who leapt to his feet and ripped the duct tape off his mouth.

Scrap walked into the dining room with Slate's pistol leveled at Corley's heart. His blue eyes held steady behind his glasses.

"Jayda, do you know where we have some rope? Or should we use the tape to tie them up?"

"Oh god," Moonbeam whispered.

"Umm … I think Leaf has twine in her art supplies," Jayda said. "I can look."

"That'll be very good. Now," he said to Corley. "I don't know if your kind dies like ours or not, but at the very least I'm betting you'll bleed."

"You won't shoot us," Corley said. "You're fake-making."

He took one step forward, challenging.

"I wouldn't do that if I were you," Scrap said.

He said it casually, as though part of him hoped that Corley would. Fann had never heard him so detached.

"You don't know what I'm capable of. Even they don't know." He gestured at the house members. "I'm not going to let you take her. But feel free to find out what happens if you try."

"She is not yours," Corley hissed, but he didn't take any more steps.

"She belongs to no one but those she chooses," Scrap said. "She chose me, and I honor that."

Breathless, Jayda tumbled into Fann, carrying a full roll of twine.

"Here," she said. "Help me."

With Scrap training the gun on Corley, Jayda and Fann tied the crow-men up as well as they could.

Fann concentrated on tying good knots. She had given them one more chance, and they had betrayed her. They were not her family anymore. They had shown her that. Blood or no blood.

When they were finished, Moonbeam plastered the bindings with duct tape, wrapping and rewrapping and wrapping again. She also slapped a new rectangle of tape over Corley's mouth. Corley glared at her, beady-sharp.

Fann doubted that tie-up job would hold for long, but at least it would give her a second to think.

"What do you want to do with them?" Scrap asked.

"I ..." She kept the gun in her eye-corner, not sure about it. "How did you know where he keeps that thing?"

"Slate trusts certain people with certain things," he said, shrugging.

"I didn't think he trusted anyone with—hold on. I just thought of something." Fann turned to the captives. "You knew I wouldn't come with you. You knew I'd made up my mind. You didn't come to apologize. So why did you come?"

Corley's eyes flashed, and Fann knew she had hit on something. She eyeballed Manak. He flinched under her look and fiddled with the hem of his shirt, then glanced out the window.

"Something's going on," Fann said.

Corley and Manak met eyes.

"Where are the rest of them?" Fann asked, an ugly squeezed feeling building in her stomach. "What are they doing?"

"You can't stop them," Manak said, with a voice-tone accepting what-was. "They are too powerful for you. You should end this silly game and come home, Fannilea. You can't win."

"I can and I will. I won't even be the first."

"You've heard Azeel's story," Manak said. He did not seem surprised.

The Murder had to know. About Slate's family. That she'd hear of Azeel. Then had the Morrigan also known?

Something about that bothered her, but she didn't have time to think what. They were trying to distract her from something, and she had to figure out what it was.

"Azeel escaped, but at what cost?" Manak said. "He spent his life alone and bitter, killing crows."

"Juanita," Fann whispered, realizing. "They went for Juanita."

Her human heart thundered as she spun toward Scrap. "We have to go! They're after Leaf again."

CHAPTER THIRTY-SEVEN

Outside the hospital, we wait.

Made-up perches, we use: roof; treelike wire-joins; gnarly-bent trees; across-the-street cars. Any working thing is ours to use.

We sit tall, with wide crow-shoulders, casting our shadows over the human sick-place. Hardlike orders from Datchett to wait and overlook, we have. Human, he is, inside with Pomo and Tek.

We wait. We overlook.

But a taxi-car below-stops, and that girl tumbles out, white-spikes and blue-ice eyes, with her new Murder behind. We stumble-wonder.

Keep her here, should we? Stop her from entering? What now?

We scold.

Wrede, seeing not Manak and not Corley, rawks above all. Warning! Not-right white-haired girl! Wrongness.

But none move to stop them. Our what-to-do from our awoah says wait.

So we wait.

Chapter Thirty-Eight

As she spilled out of the cab, Fann ducked, expecting a dive-bomb. When the crows kept their perch, she ran for the door full-pelt, her heart thundering with worry.

Datchett had left those kekking crows here. the whole Murder of them. Told them to stay. He thought he could take Leaf alone. He thought it would be easy.

"Hurry," she breathed as she, Moonbeam, Scrap, and Jayda pushed through the hospital doors. The harsh rawks of the Kaa knifed her heart even as the closing of the doors shut them out.

People cluttered the waiting room, filling every chair and spilling onto the floor. The phone-lady spoke to a big-bellied woman with a little one clinging to her, monkeylike. Children with empty-sick eyes hung from parent hands. One girl held ice in a bag to an ankle that turned the wrong way. Someone else bled from an ear.

"This is good," Fann said. "Busy. One at a time, and I don't think they will see."

Her breath held, she walked, as normal as she could, past the phone-lady. When the talk with the pregnant woman heated up, she sped up and pushed through the door into the hall of rooms. Her ears perked for a shout to stop her, but none came, and she scurry-hustled down the hall, heart pumping wild.

A squeak of shoes behind her signaled the others following, but she did not wait. Leaf needed her.

She turned the corner into her friend's room.

Human-formed Pomo and Tek had Slate by the arms, trapped between them.

"Fann!" he shouted. "He has Leaf!"

Datchett heavy-hung over Leaf, hands on her collarbone, eyes closed.

"Get away from her!"

Fann tumbled into the room and flung herself at Datchett. She slammed into him with everything she had—

—and he held straight. Fannilea crumple-fell, pain in every part. A brick wall, he was. Some kind of magic, he had.

"Fannilea," he crowed. "So nice of you to join us, but I'm afraid we can't stay. We have somewhere to be."

"You can't take her," she said, but she hardly had breath to speak.

"Ock, white-haired girl, the Murder has pinchy-peered into her soul and found her ready to journey to the Otherworld."

"It's a lie. She's not. You know it!"

Datchett wore an ugly-sweet crow-smile. He fluttered his eyelashes, love-looking from beneath drooped eyelids. "Perhaps the Murder's findings would alter ..." he almost-sang, " if the right ... *alternative* were offered."

Fann's heart fell. She knew what he wanted.

"I've contracted with the Morrigan," she said, her voice-tone flat. "I have four days left."

But the Morrigan wasn't there.

And she hadn't stood up for Fann the last time.

"The thing about the goddess, Fannilea, is that she doesn't like to be pestered with family-fighting. That contract, you ought not take it too serious. She certainly doesn't."

"You're the ones who called her in."

"For help! Not meaning to leave *everything* to her …" Datchett pressed on Leaf's throat, and she choked. "Ock, what next? Return, will you, with us? Or should we take your friend instead?"

"No!" Fann shouted. "Stop!"

"Return with us," Datchett said, "or she does." He pressed harder.

At the spot where Datchett's hands met her throat, Leaf twitched. The small movement grew, rattling her chest. It slunk into her stomach. At her pelvis it became a body-quake, shaking her legs, her ankles, her feet down to her toe-tips. The hospital bed jig-jagged.

"Leaf!" Fann shouted. She wanted to get in and stop him, but she feared to hurt Leaf more.

The shaking rose to a not-possible level, and a wispy, made-of-color form wound out of Leaf's mouth. It hovered, and the shaking stopped. Brown saucer-eyes popped wide at Fann from inside the thing's milk-like cloud. Its silver brow bent, wronglike.

"What's going on?" it said.

Datchett and Fann spoke at once, Datchett with a calm voice-tone and Fann with a make-fast one—

"I am your guide, young one. I am here to help you find your way to the next world. Do not be afraid."

"Leaf! Don't listen to him! It's not your time! Don't let him take you!"

Those saucer-eyes tried to understand. They were Leaf's, but not quite.

"What do I do?" the wisp said to Datchett.

Datchett offered his arm with a teeth-baring smile. "You must twine with me, so you will not be lost. Take my arm, and we will go."

Fann's crow-heart beat hard. The only way to stop Datchett was to muddle up the twining.

The soul might twine with Fann instead. Her hands hot-sweated at this.

Memory stole her, so much she felt the Boneman like he was here, now. The way his nothing-fingers reached into her; the wild crack of her wing as it snapped in half. Her stomach squeezed.

She couldn't do it.

But the made-of-color wisp turned saucer-eyes back to her—Leaf's eyes.

"I do not feel right. Is it right?"

This was not the Boneman. It was Leaf. Her friend.

"No," Fann whispered. "It is not right."

"Oh? Is someone going to stop me?" Datchett flicked an eyebrow, delicatelike, his arm still out. "Pomo! Tek! Might you find a song somewhere in your hearts?"

"Uh … boss?" Pomo hard-fought with Slate, who would not stay still.

"The song of fealty." Datchett's voice-tone did not sound pleased. "To help our crow-daughter remember her place."

"Of course," Tek said, and the two crow-men began to sing.

But this time, Fann was ready.

Quick-fingered, she pocket-dug for two wax lumps she had there. She stuffed one into each ear, thanks-giving to Scrap for making her wait while he dashed to his room before they left. Thanks-giving that he seemed to have right-tools at right-times.

"I will," she whispered, answering Datchett, but not for his hearing, only to make herself stronger. It echoed in her head, made round and wild and more true by the stopping of her ears.

"I will stop you," she said, louder this time.

Pomo and Tek's song buzzed and whined as they tried to bring her under. The song pounded against her crow-heart, thudding like wings against windows.

But her will was strong, and with her ears stopped, her human-heart stronger. She held herself upright, thrust her chin out, and fought back, standing fierce.

The song would not conquer her.

But Datchett did not wait; he reached for the Leaf-soul.

There was no time to be not-sure—

Fann jumped between.

CHAPTER THIRTY-NINE

Sparks flared, and the Leaf-soul cried out. Its wisps flailed. Lost in the air, they slip-slid against the skin of what had gotten in the way, and then around it, and then into it. The human crow-girl took a wild breath, and the soul wove around and along her with a gentle sigh. She let it come.

Soft as nesty feathers, it was. Wrapped in a cloud, she was—no, inside her, there. A fat, bold, sunny-day cloud, not a weeping-gray rain cloud. Warm whiteness rose, peace everywhere. She had no fear. Perfect rightness, this was.

A golden light shone in her heart, calling to her. Calling to both of them. To come home. To lie down, for it was time. Time to be at rest. At peace.

At—

No!

Fann whuffed. That was wrong!

She spoke to herself, trying to reach the Leaf-soul. "Leaf, I need you to wake up. It's not your time."

Datchett bared his teeth with a lip-curl. "It's too late. She's bound to you now. You must take her."

"Her body is still here, living. There must be some way for her to return to it."

Fann hoped.

"The others are here, too," she said aloud to her Leaf-self. "Everyone."

Fann flapped a hand at the doorway, where the house members perched. They came forward, Jayda leading, Moonbeam trailing, Scrap eyeballing Datchett. Slate beat against the crow-men's arms, and Datchett, seeing that there was nothing he could do, waved for them to let him go.

The house members gathered at Leaf's bedside.

"Now what?" Scrap said.

"I don't know," Fann said. "Talk her into staying? It was a mistake, the taking."

"Leaf!" Moonbeam pulled at the corner of the blanket. "Fann told us everything, right? She's cool with us. We're all cool. So get your little goth bootie back here and join this bad-ass house we're gonna have."

Scrap snorted. "Yah," he said. "What Moonbeam said."

"Eh! Making fun of me? But backing me up, aren't you? Like you got nothing better to do." Moonbeam shot him a mock-cross look. "Weirdo."

"Jayda?" Fann asked. "Is what Moonbeam says true? That we're cool?"

Jayda glanced down at Leaf, then back up at Fann. Her chin jutted upward. "I don't know," she said. "But I think we can sort it out."

"I can stay?" Fann whispered.

"If it's up to me." Jayda nodded.

Fann bit her lip, chewing back a smile.

"Guys?" the Leaf-soul said with Fann's voice, sounding more like Leaf now. "What's happening? I felt like … I had to go. But … I don't want to."

"No," Fann said to the Leaf-self. "You have to stay. Hurry now."

"You told them what you told me? All of them? Everything?"

"Yep."

"Slate?"

Slate stood back from the bed near the foot; now he took a delicate step, but only to the edge of the bed. He looked at Leaf-in-the-bed, not at the twined soul-thing.

"Leaf. I'm here."

"You and Fann?"

Now Slate's gray eyes slanted Fann's way.

"We have some things to talk about. We'll do that when you're home, *verdad*?"

"All right," Leaf said. "I think—"

A puff-feel of clouds gathered on Fann's skin at her cheeks and throat and hands. The form of the Leaf-soul stretched like cotton spiderwebs, wisping away from Fann, gaining its own strength. It detached gently and hovered over the hospital bed once more.

Datchett pushed forward and reached out. "Take my arm!"

But the house members stood firm against him, forming a two-strong, two-wide wall between him and Leaf. The Leaf-soul did not even look; it blew a kiss to Fann and, in an eye-blink, disappeared into the space over Leaf's throat.

The house members held their breath, waiting.

Was that pink returning to Leaf's cheeks? It was hard to tell . . .

Leaf groaned and shifted.

The house members breathed and smiled and poked each other. Moonbeam stretched her forehead so as not to cry. Scrap hummed at her.

"Leaf?" Fann said.

Leaf did not respond, but she breathed steadily, her chest rising and falling.

"This is not over," Datchett said. All smooth charm had fled. His lids lay hooded over sharp eyes smoking with rage, and his words bit, punchlike. "We will come back for you, Fannilea Ishika Fiachra. You belong to us."

Scrap turned and met Datchett's gaze, a work of stone himself. Straightlike, he said, "She doesn't. But you go ahead and come at us. We'll be ready."

Moonbeam set a hand on Scrap's shoulder. "*We're* her people now. You leave her be."

Something stirred in the back of Fann's mind. *We're her people now.* Were they? Like the Murder? It was not the same. Something about the contract—she needed to think about it. She needed a moment—

Jayda said nothing, only stepped forward, backing up Scrap and Moonbeam—and Fann.

"There is still the Morrigan," Fann said, the contract lingering at the edge of her thoughts.

She had won the acceptance of the house members. At least, she thought she had. Would the Morrigan support her now?

Datchett sneered. "Don't forget to read the fine print, nestling." He flicked a finger at Pomo and Tek, and the three crow-men disappeared through the doorway.

"He meant what he said." A cloud of disquiet darkened Slate's brow. "They'll be back for you."

"I'm sure they will," Fann said. "But—"

A massive, jaw-widening yawn overtook her.

"Sleep first," Scrap suggested helpfully.

"Uh, guys?" Moonbeam sputtered.

Everyone turned. Moonbeam sat on the edge of the bed, her hand in Leaf's, and Leaf's eyes were open.

CHAPTER FORTY

"Fann! Fann! Wake up! Fann, you have to wake up. I need to know what's going on. Wake up *now*!

Yelling. So much yelling. Stop it, they must. Her skin flamed. Burning, she was. Sweating. And itching. Oh goddess, the itching.

"It itches," she mewled. She had a terrible, terrible need to scratch. She reached back again.

"Stop! Fann, you have to stop! Wake up!"

Wasn't she awake? Hadn't she been, somewhere in the dark? Her eyes, were they open? She fought with them.

A room swam into focus. Hers, she thought. Her room. Her nest. At the house. Home. Her home.

Oh goddess, the itching.

Someone took hold of her wrists and held them hard. "Stop," he said. "You're scratching your skin off. You've had a two-hundred-degree fever for two days. Something's wrong. How do I fix it?"

"Two days?" That was bad. Two days, where had they gone? She needed them, but what for? There wasn't time. Running out, it was. Two days ...

She struggled against Slate's hold. "Let me go! My wings ..."

"Your wings? What's going on?" He spun her around.

Her T-shirt slipped, too big, falling down a shoulder, revealing the skin of her back. It was stippled with small points of red, some with black points protruding from them. They covered her shoulders and her spine, an irritated red.

"Fann ... what ..."

She reached around and scratched hard, up and down, more and more. It didn't help.

"Feathers," she said, dreamlike. "My feathers returning ... but it itches!"

"Fann, how do I stop it?"

Funny, he was, this strange stone-eyed boy. So desperate, too.

"You don't stop it," she said. "It is shek. You can't stop shek."

"There must be something ..." he mutter-wondered, and then— "Dammit! How could I forget? Stupid, stupid, stupid! Fann, where did you go?"

"Wok?"

"Where did you go, when I kicked you out? You must've stayed somewhere, left your things somewhere. Where?"

She flailed, in her memory. Somewhere, yes, but how to say? "Broken-house ... not far ..."

Oh goddess how she itched and burned, burned and itched. It hurt so much. Something she needed to do, there was, something she was saying ... something about a house ... but she could not catch it before everything went black again.

Hot liquid, on her mouth. Full of tang, like makeberries. Dripping onto her tongue ...

More. Makeberries, hot, tea.

Fann woke to warm afternoon sunlight filtering into her room at Shady House. Her blankets lay in a tangled heap at her feet.

Slate sat against the wall next to her head, eyes closed. A tea mug rested near his knee. Next to it sat the terra cotta pot she'd taken from the house. Nothing grew in it.

Apparently the Morrigan and the Murder had told the truth about some things.

"Slate," she whispered.

His eyes flew open. "Fann? How do you feel? Are you all right?"

"I ... I think so. I don't remember ...

"Show me your back."

She obeyed, trusting that he had his reasons. He laid his hand against the bare skin of her shoulder, soft and smooth and fully, normally, human. "You're OK," he said. "You didn't have the berries, and you got so sick, and I—it's my fault, because I didn't remember that you needed them, I didn't think to get them, and—"

"Ssh," she said, putting a finger to his mouth. "Stop it. Thank you."

"For?"

"For taking care of me."

"But I didn't. I kicked you out, and I—"

"You had a why, based on what you knew. Do you understand now, that they are not my people?"

"They are the *matones*. The ones *mi papi* spoke of."

"*Sí.*" She had learned this much, at least, from his mother.

"I watched you jump into the middle of some crazy magic without even thinking, without a fear, to stop that *cabrón* from taking Leaf. You think that wouldn't be enough for me to know where you stand?"

Fann closed her eyes, a warm-finally feel washing over her.

"I'm sorry I couldn't see it sooner. I blamed the destruction of my family on the Kaa and took it out on you. It wasn't your fault—or even theirs, really—that Azeel's story destroyed my mother. She's the one who let it. She's the one who gave up on us. On herself."

"Maybe then," Fann said, softlike. "Now … maybe she has changed."

"Fannilea Ishika Fiachra—that's some name, by the way—are you sticking your beak into my family's business?"

"Nope. Never. No way. Only … maybe you feel like paying her a visit. Someday."

Mock-stern gray eyes slanted at her. "Maybe. Someday."

"Good enough for me." Fann pushed herself up off the blankets. Her arms shook. "Where are the rest? I'm weak still."

"The rest? Of the berries? We used them all. We didn't know how many you needed. I—do you need more?"

Fann looked at the pot of soil, unsprouted. "It doesn't matter. There are no more, and …" She stopped, frowning. "If I needed makeberries that bad, I must've been out for a while."

"Two days."

"Two days? What day does that make it?"

"It's Monday. The thirty-first. New Year's Eve day."

The last day of her contract. Thank the goddess she hadn't slept through it! And … she had won it, hadn't she? Slate had been the last. And he had said he understood.

That was it. Leaf, first. Which reminded her—

"How is Leaf? Is she home yet?"

"No. Yesterday she said she thought they would let her check out today. Her mother's picking her up."

Then Moonbeam. Scrap. Jayda. Today, at last, Slate. She had not discussed the contract. They had accepted her, knowing what she truly was.

But Fann remembered Datchett's words: *"Check the fine print, nestling."*

What was she missing?

The contract lay stuffed in a hole in the wall in the other corner of the room. She wanted to yank it out and have a look at it—was there a detail she'd overlooked? What was the fine print? What could the Morrigan possibly use against her? But not in front of Slate. That would violate the contract. She had to be careful. No one could see her with it, still. No one could know about it.

"Fann," Slate said. "Datchett wasn't kidding. They'll be back. How do we fight them?"

"I think I have a way of dealing with them," she said.

"Fann . . ."

"I can't talk about it. There's something that might work, but if I talk about it, it goes away."

"Okay. I get it. Actually … there was something else I'd been thinking of asking you." Slate cleared his throat and played with a corner of the blanket.

Fann frowned. What could make her iron-boy fidget so?

"I wondered if we could … I mean, do you want to … go to eat? To dinner, I mean."

"To dinner?" Fann's cheeks grew warm.

"Just us, I mean, not—"

"Two alone? I see," she rushed, ducking her head.

But before she could say anything else, the bedroom door banged open, and Moonbeam burst in.

"Sorry to interrupt, love-birdie-pies, but that freaky crow-brother of Fann's is wokking like a *loco*-bird out back. Says he needs to talk to her. Says it's an e-mer-gen-see. Huge, big important e-mer-gen-see."

"He's here?" Slate said, frowning. "How can he think we would let him in?"

"I don't want to talk to him," Fann said.

"I told him that! But he won't quit. He said he has to talk to you and if you won't come down, he'll shout so that everyone hears."

Fann rolled her eyes. "Dammit, Corley." She pushed to her feet, slowlike. She wasn't quite stable.

"He's not on your side, Fann," Slate said. "It could be a trap. Let one of us go. At least to find out what he wants."

Moonbeam grimaced. "Tried that. He won't talk to anyone but her."

Fann rubbed at her forehead. "I have to see what he wants."

Slate shook his head, about to reply—when a shrill,

raucous call echoed through Fann's window, silencing all three of them.

Aw aw aw. Again and again, meant for her. *Aw aw aw*.

Fear-bumps collected along Fann's arms and the back of her neck. She knew that call; she knew what it meant among crows: It was the alert call for an approaching predator.

Corley was warning her.

CHAPTER FORTY-ONE

"I will talk to you from here! You cannot come in; I will not come out. Understand?" Fann shouted from the back door. She kept the door propped against her hip—that way she could close it super-fast if Corley tried to come in or slip out with one step if the house members were in danger.

Corley stood in the middle of the backyard, human. Wondrous strange that he could make such exactly crowlike sounds with his human voice instruments. What a singer he had always been. But now he flapped his hands and rocked from side to side and fast-muttered, endless, more to himself than to her, working out his not-knowing.

"I should not I should not I should not. It is against shek; it is against the Murder ... but ... my sister. Little Lea my sister. How to choose? Let one break the other, how?"

"Corley. What are you saying?"

His eyes quick-flicked along the edges of the yard, one edge, then the next, around and around. His fingers twittered at his thighs. He seemed unable to speak to her.

Finally, after one last check, all as one he blurted, "The Murder is coming! They are coming for you, here to this place."

Fann sighed. "I know, Corley."

"But ... you must run! They are on the way. Now!"

"I have fulfilled my contract with the Morrigan. As long as she keeps her word, I am free. All I have to do is call her."

Corley's eyes rolled like those of a scared horse, the whites showing. "Sneaking Lady! Don't trust."

"I am lost regardless. I will not go back."

"I wanted to help you still," Corley said, cheeks drooping.

"You've had many chances to help me. So many, Cor. You made your choice."

"Not a choice, not a choice," he muttered. "I have tried to say. Everyone tried to say. You did not listen. It has come to hurt you."

"You're wrong. I *do* have a choice, and I have made it. I will fight for it. Nothing they can do or say will make me go back."

"It is not do or say. It is *blood*. There is no fighting blood."

"Blood is happenstance. It is choices that matter. *That* is who we really are. I am what I made me."

Corley gawped at her. "Stray! So much, you do, from your shek. It is not good. It is not true. Shek is true."

"They've trained you well, haven't they, my crow-brother?" Fann said, falling sadlike, realizing that truly, Corley was theirs. He would not understand.

Whatever sameness had existed between them in their childhood was gone. He was of one kind, and she another—not because of blood, but because of choices. He had turned-face against her, and to protect herself and the ones she loved, she must do the same, no matter the pain it might leave.

In the coming battle, she would fight on one side, and he the other. She would have to be ready to hurt him. Even kill him, if it came to that. A waiting or a feeling of it being not-right would put herself or her dear ones in danger. She must not let that happen.

It was a simple thing—and yet. He had been her brother, once.

She wondered if things of this sort happened much among humans. How did they make-right with it? She supposed she would learn.

"One thing more," Corley said. "I brought you something. If you lose ... you will need them. You will not be able to get more. I don't know what you will do after that, but ..."

He came to her, stopping a few feet shy, and held out his clasped right hand. He let the fingers fall open, and a pile of burgundy makeberries shone in his cupped palm.

"Oh, Corley," Fann said, sighing. "It doesn't change anything."

"I know," he said. "Take them anyway. They have a strange old magic. Maybe there is something they can do for you."

Could she trust him, one last time? She close-watched him, looking for signs of trickery. There were none. She scooped the makeberries from his palm.

Once she had them, he turned around and walked back to the middle of the yard. In his shoulder-length black hair there was a gaping hole.

A light layer of fringe covered his neck, but a triangle-shaped thatch had been ripped free. The hairs around it frayed, half-broken.

"Corley ... why is there a chunk missing from your hair?" Fann put her hand up, half-thinking to explore the hole with her fingers, but he was too far to reach.

Corley dodged, turning, eyes flicking sideways. "Bad haircut," he said. "Will grow back."

"You don't get haircuts."

Fann's skin felt suddenly strange, as though it were not her own. It prickled like light skittering up and down her limbs. She wanted to rub her arms. She felt it at the back of her neck, too, tingling at her hairline, going to her head, making her feel dull and a bit dizzy. She wanted it to stop, so she could think, but it buzzed in her head, fogging her brain.

She struggled. That hair …

There was only one explanation.

"Corley. You lost some feathers, didn't you? That's why your hair looks like that."

Corley stepped back. "Fannilea," he said. He would not look at her. "Don't ask me that."

"My name is Fann," she said. "And I will ask you whatever needs asking, Corley Drust Fiachra."

She dug into her jeans pocket. They were still there— the crow feathers she had found on the night Leaf was hurt. She crushed them between her fingers.

"Corley."

"Hmm?" Now he responded with silk, but she knew him. It was a wrapping on something pointy.

"Turn crow."

Corley shook his head.

"Corley, I want to see your feathers."

"Should not have come," Corley said, his voice-tone frosted over. "You have not changed from cheepy nestling. Shek brings happpiness. Me-me wants do not. Murder does good. But you are low."

"Low because I wish to be happy? Because I will fight for it? That *is* my good thing. It is *the* good."

"Wrongness!" Corley shrieked. "You will be shown!"

Fannilea lunged and hissed at him, as she would a pest she wanted to chase off. "Get out of here, and don't come back."

Droopy-lidded, Corley turned his face away from her. It would be the last time.

He turned crow practically midair, rushing. As he hurtled into the sky, Fann caught a last glimpse of a gap in his tail the size of approximately three feathers, exactly like the ones she carried in her pocket.

Sometimes it hurt to be right.

But, in both her hearts, Fannilea knew that it hurt much worse to keep being wrong.

CHAPTER FORTY-TWO

At dusk, we fly-sneak like a great black cloud into the human world. We slice across the sky with a power-feel. Straight and true.

We are one, and that white crow is apart. She is not-right, and she must be taught. It is the way of the Murder.

Down-low, the humans feel us come. A wronglike hurt in their hearts, because this time we are here without Death. We seek-find one of our own, for lessons.

We descend as one, and we take our seat on the tree of the house. We swallow its needles with our black feathers, sharp beaks, and clawlike feet.

We do not say we are here, but perch and wait. Silence falls all around. Nothing moves or makes a sound—every last breathing-thing here knows us, feels us, and gets down lowlike. They are all afraid.

Except in that kekking house. In that house, there is movement.

CHAPTER FORTY-THREE

As soon as Corley had gone, Fann bolted upstairs. The makeberries sat heavy in her pocket, where she had stuffed them without thinking. But she didn't have time to deal with them. She had to look at that kekking contract before the Murder came.

In her bedroom, she closed the door and set a chair against it. She removed the rock that blocked the hole in the wall, yanked the contract out, and unrolled it.

She pored over the paper one word at a time. What had she missed? She found nothing. She bit her lip to keep from screaming and read it again. Still nothing. And again. And again.

It was not very long.

No matter how she tried, Fann could not find a single word out of place. Everything seemed in order. She had followed the contract to the letter and won it fair and square.

Yet something still bothered her, niggling at the edge of her mind. It wasn't Datchett's words; she was sure he was wrong.

She fingered the corner of the parchment, staring at the dusky red of her bloody thumbprint.

What a thing it was, to hinge her whole future on the acceptance of strangers. It didn't seem fair. Not-right . . .

Her thoughts were interrupted by a hard-pressing against her brain. The Murder had come; she sensed them.

She stuffed the contract in her pocket and hopped downstairs to the kitchen. Out the window, the blackened tree and thickening night set her pulse racing. Vaguely, she thought she should find a weapon.

Slate found her standing over the junk drawer, staring into it.

"Hey," he said gently. "Come out of there."

She let him take her elbow and turn her. Together they faced the dining room and the dark tree beyond. Fann saw that Slate had the gun tucked into his waistband, but she did not comment.

Jayda came down shortly after and took up Fann's left side, her eyes icy. She may not have been sure at first, but she had made her decision, and now she would defend it.

As was their habit, Moonbeam and Scrap came down together.

Scrap handed Fann a new pair of earplugs, and Fann grimly stuffed them into her ears.

Moonbeam handed her a pair of pink fuzzy earmuffs.

"Wear these, too. Just in case."

"Moonbeam—"

"Don't you argue with me, crow-face."

Fann smiled faintly, draping the earmuffs on her arm.

"I'll put them on later if I have to."

Moonbeam saluted her with pretend honor, and Fann glimpsed something shiny-silver strapped to her bicep—a switchblade. She raised an eyebrow at her friend, and the girl shrugged.

"I lived on the street for a while. I know how to use it."

Fann did not doubt it.

But she did doubt whether this ragtag group of semi-orphans could defeat the Murder. Especially if the Morrigan did not support her.

It frightened her, but what could she do now? She had made her choices, and she did not regret them. She had to let the others make theirs as they would. She raised her chin and set her shoulders, ready for what the Murder would bring.

It did not take long.

As night descended on the end of a year in New York City, a lone crow flew out of the Shady House pine tree. Slightly larger and slightly rounder than the rest, it had spindly legs, glinting black eyes, and an all-too-familiar swoop in its flight. In its beak fluttered something that glowed white against the dark. The crow landed on the windowsill and bobbed its head, waving the white thing.

"What is that?" Scrap asked.

"A bit of tissue?" Moonbeam answered.

"It's a white flag," Fann said faintly.

"We're not letting him in here," Slate said.

"Or you out there," Jayda added.

Two other crows flew from the tree to the window, each holding one end of a piece of paper in their beaks. They hovered, flapping, in front of the window.

Fann read what the paper said.

I KNOW WHO YOUR FATHER IS.

A searing pain gripped her chest. She felt as though she'd been stabbed. Her father? When had she last thought of her parents? She had kept them out of her head, for so long, on purpose, that to think of them now made her short of breath.

They had left her. Long ago. And never cared to reclaim her. What did it matter?

But she could not deny her curiosity. Of course Datchett knew. The whole Murder surely knew.

"My father," she said.

She had thought she wouldn't care, and in a way, she was still not sure she did. But her story did not have a beginning. It wasn't so much that she wanted to know *him*, but that she wanted to *know*.

This would be her last chance to find out. Lose it, and she would never know.

"Fann," Slate said steadily. "It's a trick. It has to be. You know him."

"Yes. Maybe. But … what if I never find out?"

"What if you don't? What does your father mean to you? What did he ever mean to you? You are not defined by him. Not in any way. Let it go."

"Do you think that's possible?"

"Yes," he said firmly. "I think you've already done it."

"You don't need them! You've got us!" Moonbeam said, threading her arm through Fann's.

"And even if you didn't," Scrap said quietly. "You'd make it on your own."

"I think you're right, Shady House. But ... if I want to talk to him ... if I want to take the chance to know ... would you help me?"

The house members looked at each other.

"I'm well protected, aren't I?" Fann coaxed. "I have earplugs and earmuffs and a bunch of the strongest, craziest, most true friends a person could ask for. Let him in."

Slate made eye contact with each of the others, one at a time. When each had nodded, some with worried looks at Fann, Slate set his mouth grimly and opened the storm door a crack.

"You—only you—can come in to speak with Fann," he said to the crow on the sill. "You will come in as crow and change to human in here. If you harm a hair on the head of anyone in this house, I will kill you. Understand?"

Datchett croaked.

Slate looked to Fann, and she nodded.

Shaking his head, Slate wedged himself between the two doors and pushed the screen door open just wide enough for a crow to hop through.

Datchett whuffed, clearly displeased. Still, he flew down and hopped inside.

Slate shut the door, narrowly missing clipping off the crow's tail feathers.

Datchett paused, turned, and shot Slate a sharp look. Fann could have sworn she heard a sniff. Then Datchett turned back and continued his hops. Two more bounces and he turned to human.

Straightening his pinstripe vest, the awoah of the Murder strutted into the dining room. He took his time, ignoring the house members, intent on Fann, who had retreated to the living room sofa.

"Fannilea," he purred. "We are here to take you home."

"You said you know who my father is. Tell me."

"We aren't angry, crow-girl."

"Do you or do you not know who he is?"

Datchett sighed. "He wants you to come back."

"Then why did he abandon me?"

Datchett settled onto the sofa next to her, leaning back, crossing one leg over his knee. "There were … complications. He had his reasons."

Fann's steely glare did not waver. "You came here to tell me something. Stop stalling and tell it."

He leaned in, trying to catch her eyes with his, which sparkled with the power of the secret. "If you think you're ready …"

His breath trailed off, and he waited.

Her face did not change.

Finally he gave up, sighing. He glanced at the house members, shifted his weight, licked his lips, and said, "All right."

Still nothing from Fann.

"All right! It's me. I'm your father, Fannilea."

CHAPTER FORTY-FOUR

Somehow, it did not surprise her. Back-looking, she wondered if she had guessed underneath. It made sense. Only the awoah could get away with having her shunted off.

"I brought these." Datchett reached into his inner jacket pocket and removed three small white feathers. "Manak gave them to me when you were small, so that I would have something of you."

"Who is my mother?"

"That's not my secret to tell," Datchett said.

"What difference could it make now?"

"It's her decision. If she tells you, you will understand why I could not."

"I don't understand any of it. You … didn't care if I lived or died."

"That's not true," Datchett said, smoothlike.

Smooth was flat, Fann thought. Not letting the thing matter.

"Of course I cared."

She listened for the sound of truth, but all she heard was a careful-stepping voice-tone. Datchett saying what he thought she wanted him to. So that she would do what he wanted her to do.

As it had ever been.

"Ock, child, you must understand. I had to consider the Murder. I had to consider my *position*. It did not matter what I wanted. The Murder would not have it. You were a bad omen, and I as their awoah would have been first not-right and then done-with. They wanted to leave you, Kaa nestling, in the human world; you would not have lived. Hard enough to stop that, it was. I fought for you."

His voice-tone pled.

"As you grew, I wanted to tell you, but how could I? I had to treat you the same. If I had said, with those"—he shook his head—"not-right white feathers, it would have torn our people apart. I had to think of the Murder."

"And now?" Fann said. "If I returned with you? Would I go as your daughter? Would you make-right with me now?"

"Ah-ha!" Datchett said, with a joyous voice-tone. "I knew it! Of course!" He became quietlike. "You may return with true-honors as my daughter and next-in-line. But you must understand, of course, that you will have to show the Murder you've changed. They will never accept you as—"

"Next-in-line?" Fann struggled to focus. Talking to Datchett clouded her brain. He never came at anything straight and true, quite.

"Fortunately you would have lots of time to show them; I don't expect to pass for some time. You can do it. You have a strong will and a biglike personality. They will believe you, when you show them."

"You are suggesting that I would ... become awoah?"

"You ..." Datchett's eyes dimmed. "But isn't it what you wanted?"

"You thought I knew it. For how long?"

Datchett raised his hands, palms up. "I thought, when you were young, and so ... hard-to-manage ..."

"That I was doing it so you would claim me and make me your next-in-line?"

"You don't *want* to be the most powerful crow in the Ahk? To be the source of wisdom your people turn to? To stand above them?" His eyebrows drove to a V. "How can that be?"

Fann's stomach twisted. Power was all he understood. Just another way of being tied to the Murder's wants and needs and thoughts. Of being lost in the group until there was nothing left of *you*.

Though knew she would not understand, she said, for her own sake, "I don't want to be crow. I don't want to stand above or below. I want to be human, and

343

I want to be free to make something of myself as I choose."

"Fannilea ..." The sparkle died. Datchett's eyes turned lost and not-sure.

"What about Corley?" she asked, for that was the last thing she needed answered. "You protected him, didn't you? When I asked to see the feathers."

"Of course."

"Did you know what he had done?"

"I had maybe-thoughts."

"Did you even consider giving him up?"

"Of course not. Not any more than I would think of giving you up."

"How did you do it? I looked so closelike at his feathers. I couldn't see anything wrong."

"The Morrigan offered feathers from her raven's tail; she painted them white with the stripe in her hair."

Fann fought to keep her chin high. That sneaky Lady! What would this mean for her contract? But she mustn't let Datchett see fear. "If that is so, then she must have had her reasons," she said. "And now, it is time for you to go."

"You're not ... you won't come with me?"

"No." She stood.

"But ... but ..." Datchett spluttered. "I'm your father!"

"Slate?" Fann called.

Datchett's eyes hardened to stone-cold. "You're going to regret this, nestling. You think you can win against me? You will find what it truly means to lose."

Slate hovered, tense and ready to come in between. "Fann?"

"Datchett was just leaving."

"My daughter is coming with me."

"No, she isn't." Hands on hips, Jayda glared.

Moonbeam growled, "Don't you touch her."

"We will fight you to the death for her. Sir," Scrap said, blue eyes fierce behind his glasses.

Datchett cocked his head with dim confusion. "But why? She is not of your Murder."

"We chose her," Slate said.

"Blood cannot be escaped. The Murder will do what it must."

"You're their leader," Slate said. "You could stop it."

Datchett looked down his nose at Slate, eyes moist with superiority. His mouth puckered in a patronizing half smile.

"Shek is the way, and we must obey."

Fann couldn't tell if he truly believed it or if he meant to say it with irony.

Light from the Christmas tree shone in rotating colors on Datchett's face—green, then red, then blue—and the strange, shifting shadows lent his nose and mouth a beaky, sinister look.

Fann stepped toward him, and the light reflected on her face in the same pattern. Green, red, blue. Green, red, blue. But Fann's icy blue eyes showed an open, knowing determination.

"Since nestlinghood I've heard the Murder say that. Like it must be so. Like it is the way it is. But why? None among you asks that. I couldn't live without asking it. What sense does it make? Why should I spend my life on your shek? What is the reason for it? I did not find one.

"I saw, as I asked, what your shek does to questioners. Thought-stopping. Thrown in a crow-prison. Force against me, one of your own, for asking questions. You hide from the truth behind your wall of shek. The truth is, shek is *not* higher than one man. Nothing is.

"I will find my own happiness. Unshackled from make-you-do. Choosing my ties. Trading for worth-things. One, alone and apart, finding-her-way, that is what is right and true."

Datchett's tongue darted across his lips. His eyelids flickered; his mouth pursed in an imitation of a smile.

"You may be right, Fannilea Ishika Fiachra," he said. "You will see how little it matters."

Datchett threw his arms up, both at once, and his body juddered. The change swept over him, but something about it wasn't right.

The pressure in the room shifted. Fann's ears popped, and her skin pressed against her bones as though the air had been sucked from around her. A distant crackle filled her ears, but she couldn't tell if it was real or her imagination.

Datchett did not shrink. He stood before them, man-sized, but ...

There came a crack and a series of crunches, and Datchett wailed, a high-pitched scream. Feathers sprouted from his shoulders, along his arms, and from his fingertips. They fluffed from the top of his head in the shape of a great crest and appeared along his cheekbones around his eyes.

His nose lengthened and narrowed, keratin forming where flesh had been. A piece of black bone curved down, a second curved up; together they clacked, meeting like pincers. But the beak did not stop there—it continued to grow up and out at the top, forming a strange gray barnacle. The growth swelled, bulging outward until it obscured Datchett's vision.

Fann had seen this type of deformity on regular crows in the human world. Scientists thought it was a reaction to environmental toxins. She thought that whatever poisons had caused it in Datchett had not come from the kind of toxins the scientists meant. Murder-poison, more like.

Fascinated by his strange transformation, Fann examined her old awoah. He looked nothing like the crow she had known. Or perhaps he was what he had always been, and she hadn't *let* herself know it. Thought-stopped, she had, like a good Kaa. There would be no more of that.

Only one thing had not changed—his eyes.

Those beady black eyes, crow eyes. She had never trusted them. How could you? Bright but devious. Always with the wild, dark planning.

She stepped back, out of the light of the Christmas tree, keeping her eyes trained on him. What would this new creature do? Did he have some different way to torture her?

The Bird-Man turned its head, fixed its pointy gaze direct on Fann, and opened its beak so wide she could see not only its tongue, but also its syrinx beyond.

Then, the Bird-Man began to sing.

CHAPTER FORTY-FIVE

A surge of triumph seized Fann's heart. Hadn't they already tried the kekking song? She had defeated it! What she had done before, she could do again.

But as the notes of the song rose in volume and power, the back of Fann's neck prickled. Something was different. Something had changed.

Datchett's voice, coming from the Bird-Man, did not sound like his own.

This was no ordinary Datchett ... this ...

An ancient power resonated from him. Her bones buzzed with it. She smelled it, like a great dusty thing —as though a centuries-old sarcophagus had been opened and the shut-up air of all that time had been released beneath her nostrils. It felt like death; she wanted to stop breathing.

Trepidation fluttered in her human heart.

Corley joined, and then Manak. Then the others, and Fann could not tell one voice from the next, and she could not find the triumph she had felt a moment before, though she scrabbled after it, grasping, as the song marched toward her.

She felt it come.

"They're singing again," Jayda whispered beside her. "But it sounds ... different. Bigger, somehow. Older."

Fann could barely hear her. The song beat like a heart in her mind. She felt it close; it was her own crow-heart, calling. She had not answered it in so long.

It coaxed her. It whispered of a perfect world. It promised a golden bliss. She could have it, with the right way. The song.

She must follow the song.

The ancient song.

It was in her bones, in her blood, in her mind, and she must go.

Datchett held out his hand.

Fann took a step toward him.

"Fann!" Moonbeam shrieked. "Put the goddamn earmuffs on!"

Something tugged on her arm. Something furry clamped onto her ears.

But whatever it was was not Fann's concern. She must answer the call. The song within her.

She took another step toward Datchett.

"She's still hearing it," Scrap said desperately. "What can we do?"

"Sing," Slate said, laughing maniacally.

Jayda's eyes widened. "That stupid song! Really?"

"It's worth a try," Scrap said.

Slate had already started, at the top of his lungs. Scrap jumped in, followed by Moonbeam and Jayda.

Scrap sang off key. Moonbeam's voice trembled with fear. Slate stumbled on the words, forgetting. They were so out of sync that each house member might as well have been singing a different song. As music, it was terrible.

But as self-defense against crows, it was something else.

Fann turned to the house members, caught. Was there something she'd forgotten? What had she been doing? She took a step back. Her heart broke. She was two people, herself and not-herself.

"It's working," Jayda rushed. "Keep singing."

"Dunno," Scrap said. "She doesn't look so good."

The color drained from Fann's face, and her brow glistened with sweat. The desire to move toward Datchett yanked at her, strong as a physical thing pulling her forward, but something about the other singing kept her rooted. Her chest constricted; she couldn't draw breath. She wanted to go out. She wanted to stay in. She wanted—to explode! At least then, would the confusion end?

The singing of the Murder rose above that of the house. It filled its ancient lungs with magic and beat back the struggling human song. The makeberries in her pocket thrummed with it. Against the beauty of the Het Ket Wok Aw Aw, the Shady House song was no match. The Murder crooned while the House croaked.

Fann had to go.

She didn't like it; she knew there was something wrong about it, but she couldn't stand the tension. It was ripping her in half. She had to do something.

She yanked the earmuffs from her head and dug the earplugs from her ears and flung them both away.

Her crow voice rose, answering the call of the Het Ket Wok Aw Aw, and she opened her beak-mouth to sing—

A hand stopped her mouth. Over the hand, Slate's gray eyes met her confused blue ones, steady and intent.

"Fann," he said. "You're staying."

"I want to," she said desperately, clawing at him, unsure whether she was trying to hang on and stay or to get him off her so she could go. "But the song . . ."

"Try this."

He reached up to his neck and lifted a black cord over his head. From the cord hung the makeberry juice–covered feather of the Morrigan, wrapped in the hair of Azeel's love Juanita.

"The pendant," Fann gasped. "You're wearing it."

"You told me to."

"You weren't going to listen!"

Slate's lips twitched, an amused not-quite-smile struggling to form. He reached up and slipped the black cord over her head.

The voices of the Murder fell silent.

The quiet rang in her ears—but also in her mind and heart. She breathed a heavy sigh of relief, and the tension in her face smoothed.

"It worked," Slate said. "You don't hear them."

"No."

She wondered. Was it only the feather? Or something else? There seemed a power in the way Slate looked at her as he slipped the pendant over her head. Standing with her against the Murder, because he understood. Maybe the power of the symbol was not so much in the symbol itself, but in the meaning it held for the bearer and in how far she was willing to go to protect the thing behind that meaning.

She didn't know, but oh how glad she was to be herself again.

"I'm all right," she said. "You can stop singing."

"Oh thank the ever-living stars!" Moonbeam threw her arms around her and squeezed so hard Fann almost choked.

"But—"

"No buts! Hush!"

"I have to go out there."

"No, you don't," Slate said. "Let them sing all night."

"We'll all wear earmuffs to bed," Scrap added.

But Fann was not going to argue. There was nothing else for it. It was her fight.

She crossed to Datchett. "You, giant crow-face, come with me." Without waiting, she pushed through the door and faced the crows in the backyard. Datchett followed.

The pine in the backyard swayed with the weight of the Murder. As Fann stood on the stoop, staring them down, unaffected by their song, the Murder slowly stopped singing, one by one. She did not see who closed his beak first, but she thought it might have been Corley.

When they had all fallen silent, she spoke.

"You have two choices. You can leave peacefully on your own and never bother me again. Or we can summon the Morrigan, who I'm sure is eager to enforce my contract." In her clutching fingers, buried in her pocket, the parchment crackled.

Shifty-footed, the crows turned.

Datchett walked out to join them. Then he raised a wing, and again the Murder opened beaks.

Singing.

Why? They knew it wouldn't affect her.

The door slammed open.

"Fann!" Moonbeam screamed. "Something's happening to Jayda!"

Fann tore back into the house.

The house members stood in a half-circle in the dining room, tension in every muscle. Jayda lay on the floor in front of them.

"What do we do?" Moonbeam asked, hands to her mouth.

Jayda's eyelids lay half-closed, the whites of her eyes still showing, milky and blank. Her neck slammed one way, then the other, her head flopping dangerously. She moaned, a low, hollow sound.

Fann recognized that moan. It was the sound of death.

"Those bastards! They're trying to take her. While she's alive!" Horror rang in her voice.

Fann knelt at Jayda's side and leaned over her. "Jayda! I'm right here; do not go anywhere. They can't do this."

Jayda showed no sign of hearing her. Her face contorted with pain, and she writhed, hips arching, back rising off the floor.

Fann could think of nothing else.

"Morrigan!" she screamed. "Goddess, decider of Life and Death! Ruler over wars! Morrigan, queen of the Otherworld! *Where are you?*"

CHAPTER FORTY-SIX

She comes as Mist, she does. She creeps along grass and under fences. She shrouds the yard until nothing can be seen. She caresses our tree, and we shudder.

We do not want her there.

Mist hangs heavily on feathers and dampens wings. She drags on us, but we keep to singing, barely. Our anthem trembles, but still our awoah does not signal a stopping, and so on we go.

The Mist crawls up the side of the Bird-Man and slicks his feathered face. She gathers along the ridges of his beak, getting in his eyes.

Still he stands firm.

Must obey the Lady! Our feathers bristle.

The Mist presses, but we sing.

Before long, the Mist leaves us. But we are not empty-headed enough to think this means we have won.

The Morrigan appears, there in the yard, pale-skinned and raven-haired, her white curl bold against the city night. Her black tresses blow wild though there comes no wind.

A heavy sword hangs in a leather scabbard at her hip. Brass-plated armor covers her shoulders and chest. It has the dullness of well-worn metal, and scratches and dents litter its surface. A scarlet-brown stain spreads across the shoulder. The Morrigan has been asked many times what it is. She never answers. Still, she does not clean it from her armor.

Appearing overhead, her ravens swoop to land on her shoulders. They glare.

"Enough!" the Morrigan roars. "Leave the human girl, for the moment. We must settle this proper."

We fall silent.

CHAPTER FORTY-SEVEN

The back door of Shady House opened, and the once crow-girl emerged. Her white hair flew helter-skelter, a violent mess, but her blue eyes held steady.

Behind her, the house members shuffled out. Jayda leaned on Slate, a bit groggy, but awake.

"Datchett!" the Morrigan commanded.

The Bird-Man stepped forward and made a simpering bow.

"Oh, cut it. You've been too free with your power of late. Remember yourself."

Datchett's black eyes gleamed fiercelike, and Fann knew he wanted to snap his beak at the goddess, but instead he said, "Yes, Lady. We are your servants."

"Better. As for you," she turned to Fann. "You needn't have summoned me in such an unpleasant manner. I was on my way."

"You were *late*. They were hurting Jayda! Why didn't you come when I completed my contract?"

The Morrigan tilted her head, her eyes inscrutable.

A bit crow-ish, Fann thought.

"Your contract has another half an hour on it, if I count human hours correctly. You have until midnight tonight."

"But . . ." Fann said, trepidation fluttering in her throat. "It's finished."

"You're allowed to call it early, if you like. Do you want to?" The Morrigan's words lofted, full of air.

Something about that tone bothered Fann. She yanked the contract out of her pocket, unfolded it, and stared at the words on the page.

"The contract stipulated that each of the house members had to accept me once they discovered what I truly was. They have." Fann's thoughts raced backward. "Leaf, Moonbeam, Scrap, Jayda, Slate. As per the terms, I did not talk about the contract. So, it's finished."

"Fann." The Morrigan's voice barely rose above a whisper. "You have a half an hour."

"So *that's* why you were being so weird," Scrap said. "You had to sign some kind of hairy fairy deal with a"—he looked the Morrigan up and down—"untrustworthy witchy-thing."

Fann wasn't sure, but she thought the Morrigan might have rolled her eyes. "Yes, Scrap," she said. "It was the only way to win my freedom. I had to get all of you to accept me, once you knew what I was." To the Morrigan, she said, "Why are you toying with me? It's ended."

"You will force my hand?" The Morrigan's cheeks clenched.

"Wait," Jayda said, reaching out to Fann. "You needed each of us? Everyone in the house?"

Fann nodded. "You're all here! Obviously—" Except they *weren't* all there. Leaf wasn't there.

What had Leaf said before she'd been hit by the car?

"You're not counting Leaf."

The Morrigan's eyes flicked up and down Fann's face.

"I cannot count her if she did not weigh in."

"She did weigh in! She said it was all right! She just wanted to go for a walk to think a bit, to process, and then …"

But Leaf had not come home from that walk.

She had not said anything more than, "It's all right."

"She said it was all right," Fann said, but her voice quavered.

"Would you take that for acceptance?" the Morrigan asked quietly. "Would you expect me to?"

"Where is Leaf?" Fann asked the house members, her heart tight.

"Her mother took her to Westchester this morning," Slate said. "She won't be back for a few days. She texted me, but with everything happening, I didn't think to—"

"It's not your fault," Fann said, because she could not say that it was all right. It wasn't.

"I'll call her now," Slate said, already turning for the house. "There's nothing in that stupid piece of paper that says she has to be *here*, is there?"

"No," Fann said, but she looked back to the Morrigan all the same.

The Morrigan nodded, ever so slight. "Let it not be said that the Lady refuses human ways of talk. If the last girl agrees by voice, it will suffice."

Slate returned with his phone to his ear. "C'mon, c'mon," he said. "It's ringing."

Fann stepped up to her tippy toes, the tension too big to keep inside without movement.

Slate shook his head. "Leaf! Call me as soon as you get this, will you? I mean, like right away, okay? We really need you for something here at the house. Fann really needs you for something. I want to hear you ringing me as soon as I hang up. OK? Talk to you soon."

Slate ended the call, his expression dark. "She's not good about paying attention to her phone," he said.

"She leaves it on vibrate, and sometimes she doesn't even look at it for hours."

Fann looked at the contract. The scratchy black words, the bloody thumbprints. She hated the thing. Was that it, then? The Morrigan would get her on a technicality?

It wasn't fair.

She gripped the parchment between two hands and thought about ripping it straight down the middle. A thrill of satisfaction zipped through her. Why did that feel so right?

The kekking contract … no, it wasn't fair. But it wasn't only her losing it that wasn't fair, was it? There was something else. If she had won, would that have made it fair?

Her thoughts spun in circles. The phone didn't ring. Time ticked away.

Slate called Leaf again, but hung up with a frustrated groan when it went to voicemail a second time.

"What do we do?" Moonbeam said.

Fann had no answer for her.

CHAPTER FORTY-EIGHT

The minutes slipped away.

Fann watched from the doorway as Scrap tried to reason with the Morrigan. The goddess watched him with an amused slant to her eyebrow. Every second that Slate's phone didn't ring left her heart jumping higher into her throat.

It was only a couple of minutes to midnight. Leaf had not called back. Whatever happened now, Fann would have to accept it. She kept staring at the contract, willing herself to see what bothered her about it. There must be something …

A clatter at the door distracted her. A voice with a high note of desperation called, "Let me *through!*"

Fann turned. Hands appeared, pushing their way between Slate and Scrap. A mop of tangled black hair, even more disheveled than usual, followed the hands, and from beneath it, her skin even paler than usual, poked the thin face and liquid-saucer eyes of the chickie-lion girl, Leaf.

"Fann, I have to tell you something!" she wheezed, almost breathless.

Fann had never been so happy to see anyone in her life. "Slow!" she said. "You're weak."

"I want you to stay! With us. In the house. With me. I mean, I know what you did for me in the hospital. But even before that. You're my friend because you're honest and curious and sharp and you liked my silly garden and you try so hard all the time at everything. None of that changes because of where you came from or what you were born as."

Fann pulled her friend into her arms. As she held her, though, something niggled at the back of her mind.

"Leaf," she said slowly. "What made you come back? Here, now? Weren't you on your way to Westchester with your mother?"

"*Her*. What's she doing here? Who is she?" Leaf thrust her chin toward the Morrigan. "She appeared in my dream. Looking just like that. She told me you needed me. When I woke up, I remembered that we hadn't talked after you told me your secret. It seemed important to tell you what I thought right away."

Fann frowned. A dream of the Morrigan, in time to arrive moments before it was too late? It seemed too good to be true. Could the Morrigan have visited Leaf? But why would she help Fann? Earlier she had seemed determined to get in the way.

"That is good enough for you, then?" Fann asked.

"You would think, wouldn't you?" the Morrigan returned coolly. "Except—time's up."

"You can't be serious," Slate said, though Fann somehow did not feel surprised.

"The stipulations of the contract are clear. Would you like me to read them to you? 'The undersigned shall complete the whole of the aforementioned tasks by no later than the witches' hour, known as midnight in the land of the living, on the sixteenth day, known as December thirty-first in the land of the living, and not a moment later.'" The Morrigan quoted verbatim without looking at the parchment clutched in Fann's trembling hand. "She's late."

"By two minutes? Ten? I've done what you asked! Everything! Even though—"

Fann scratched at her face, uncertain, and found her cheek wet. The backs of her eyes hurt.

"Even though?"

"It's not—you can't—" Fann fought for clarity. "You never intended to uphold it. It was all a trick."

The Morrigan closed her eyes. "So quick to assume the worst of your goddess."

"You're not being fair. I completed the contract."

The Morrigan's eyes flew open, and in their darkness flashed anger—and something else, something Fann couldn't identify.

"No, I'm not. But you'll find that that's often true in your precious human world. This place you'd so desperately like to claim as your own isn't like the Ahk, where everything is decided and set in motion for you and all you have to do is take your place. If you were to live here, you would have to be able to deal with some wicked forms of injustice."

Fann looked at the contract again. "You know," she said. "That may be true. But here, I have choices. Here I can make things as fair as possible, as far as they are under my control. And if I had understood that before, I don't think I would have signed this contract."

Fann held the parchment up, gripping it between two hands. Then she ripped it in half.

CHAPTER FORTY-NINE

Fann put the pieces of the contract together, turned it, and ripped again. She ripped again and again and again, until it was nothing but shreds. Then she stretched out her arms and loosed her fists, fingers splaying, and the scraps of paper fluttered through the air and drifted to the ground.

Scattered there, they looked to her like a new beginning.

The Murder did not whisper, as they were wont to in situations like this. They simply blinked and blinked, otherwise as still and silent as plaster-cast crow statues.

Fann thought she heard a gasp from one of the house members. Moonbeam.

The Morrigan's expression was unreadable. It looked like a mix of emotions, but Fann couldn't identify any of them. The goddess gazed at the torn pieces of paper as though they were the last remnants of the body of a loved one, but there was something besides grief in her eyes, something odd. Was it … pride?

"That thing"—Fann pointed at the shreds of the contract—"should never have existed."

And this, she knew now, was what had been bothering her all along. She hadn't been able to see it, but, with the Morrigan threatening to take her life from her, she understood.

"This human-group has a good feel with me and they have accepted my strangeness. It is good. But … what if it were not? So many smalllike things, all theirs, none mine, could have made me not-win that contract. What if they had been not-this-way? What if they had not liked me for having been born part crow and had closed their hearts and minds to me? Or what if they had not liked me for who was around me instead of my own-self? The Murder brought them harm! They might have thought I was the nestling of my crow-family—which tried to kill their dear friend—and thrown me out. What if these five had been too busy to spend their thoughts on me? They might have been living their own lives and not caring.

"I could not make changes to that. It was not mine to have say over, only theirs. Your blood contract held me to their wants. It made *my* life hang on *their* feels and thoughts. In place of shek, the contract put the human-group's feels about me. It took my life out of my decisions, same as the Murder. But I want to live here, in the land of the living, because it's not that way. Here, I may hunt for truth, no matter what others think—of it or of me. Here, my life depends on no one else's thoughts or feels or wants or anything! Here, I am responsible for my own-self. I am in charge of my living. That is what it means to live here, and that is far more than that piece of paper ever meant."

Fann met the raven-haired Lady's gaze.

A slight smile graced her lips, and that look, the odd one, had not left.

She could not possibly be proud of Fann. There must be some misinterpretation. It was something else.

The Morrigan pursed her lips and tilted her head, and her eyes went misty, as though she were remembering something from long ago.

Kek, she was a beautiful woman. Her long, straight nose; her pale, almost translucent skin; her dark but brilliant eyes; her high cheekbones and sharp chin; her wide, unfriendly mouth—as Fann looked, the Morrigan turned her face away, to the side, so that Fann could not look into her eyes, and something about the gesture, something about the way she looked from the side like that ... in an eye-blink, Fann saw herself.

It was a trick of the light, she thought. It couldn't be.

It lasted only a moment. Then, the smile disappeared and the goddess's eyes turned to steel.

"You give me no choice, then, crow-daughter," she said. "For, Fannilea Ishika Fiachra, you have not satisfied the requirements of the contract and you are in violation of your shek. You must return to the Ahk with your Murder."

Fann's heart dropped out through her stomach. So the Morrigan would betray her after all. Her hands shook.

"I will not go," she whispered.

"Very well," the Morrigan said. "Then I shall have to make you."

As the Morrigan raised her arm, palm out, fingers splayed, Slate raised the pistol and aimed it at the Morrigan's heart.

CHAPTER FIFTY

At the sound of the gun firing, the Murder burst into the sky.

Everything happened so fast—Fann turned back to the Morrigan, waiting for her to be hit, but she kept standing there with her arm raised, hair blown by an unseen wind, her grim steely gaze fixed on Slate.

A sunk-low, deep-in-the-stomach grunt pulled Fann's attention back to Slate—

—in time to see him thrust backward by the force of the bullet he had fired.

It took him on the upper left side of his chest. He stumbled, eyelids drooping, and crumpled to the ground.

Dimly, Fann heard sounds—people screaming, the Murder nattering, her own teeth grinding. She saw the house members move forward. She saw the Morrigan lower her arm, a self-satisfied smile showing on her lips but not in her eyes. She watched the crows flap their wings, and she knew that the wind blew tonight in a southeasterly direction, so it should be in her face, but she felt nothing. The world had receded, and there was nothing but her slow, slow thoughts.

A voice filtered in, with words Fann did not want to hear.

"He ... he's not breathing," Jayda said, from somewhere near the ground.

"He's dead," the Morrigan said.

The goddess's strident voice crashed into Fann's numb world, and the crow-girl struggled to keep it out. She thought of Slate's unyielding gray eyes, that day on the rooftop, how much he'd hated her—perhaps if she could think of him hating her, it would make it easier, perhaps if she could hold onto that, he would not look so gone …

"You must mean a great deal to him. Look," the Morrigan said, and the steel was gone, replaced by awkward gentleness. She pointed behind Fann.

There in the center of the house members, above the spot where Slate's body lay, rose a faint wisp of iridescent glimmer. It had little substance; Fann could barely see it. But it shimmered there in the air, hovering, a faint wobbly shape.

"The Murder will be called to riik," the Morrigan said.

"No! There must be another way."

The Morrigan gazed at her through slitted eyes. "There might be. You can guess."

Fann gritted her teeth. "Say it."

"Return to the Murder. Assume your true duty, and follow your shek."

The world seemed to tilt. Would they stop at nothing?

She crumpled next to Slate's empty body, his soul barely hanging on. She felt the pieces of herself float to the ground the way the scraps of contract had.

"I cannot live without you," she whispered into his neck. "And I cannot live with them."

"There must be some other way," Leaf said.

Something squished against Fann's stomach. She reached into her pocket. The makeberries Corley had given her leaked warm juice on her fingers.

Giving makeberries to a human was forbidden. No one had ever said why. She had assumed it was for their own good, but now, as she remembered the story of Azeel, she wondered. Grieving over his lost love, Juanita. Eating makeberries. Kissing her mouth, one last time. She had breathed—hadn't she?

She pulled her hand out of her pocket with a fist full of makeberries; they gleamed a deep burgundy, an unnatural sheen on their plump skins. They squished to juice in her palm with just one squeeze.

"What are you doing?" the Morrigan hissed.

Fann held her fist to Slate's mouth and let the makeberry juice drip through her fingers onto his lips.

Jayda, seeing what she was doing, knelt down and gently tilted his chin to open his mouth. Makeberry juice trickled onto his tongue.

"Stop!" the Morrigan shrieked. "Stop that, or—"

"Or what?" Fann said dangerously. "I'm going to die. I will not return to the Murder. You will not let me stay. The person I love the most is dead. What is left for me to live for? Shek?"

Fann let the rest of the makeberry juice drip into Slate's mouth.

"Then you are certain," the Morrigan said. "You would give up your crow essence. For him?"

"You know I would. But not for him. For me."

The Morrigan studied her with reluctant but approving eyes. Was there resignation there? Pride again? Fann wasn't sure.

She had done all she could. Now it was up to the goddess.

With the flick of an eyebrow, and the twitch of a lip into an almost-sneer, the Morrigan, chooser of victors and losers in battle, decider of fates, queen of Life and Death, gave in.

Chapter Fifty-One

The goddess turned to Datchett.

"Human, body and soul, this girl is. Forcing her to return to the Murder would only weaken it. Instead she shall surrender her crowness and remain here"—a cheer went up among the house members, and Fann's lip twitched—"as a human. She will no longer be of the Murder. Instead she must make her own way as a regular human in the human world."

"Done a good job on that already," Scrap muttered—though he was sharply elbowed and hushed by Moonbeam.

But the Morrigan only turned back to Fann, with a smile like a cat who'd caught a bird.

Definitely pride.

But before Fann had time to wonder, the goddess moved next to her.

"I will take your crowness, then, white-feathered one," she whispered.

"What do I do?"

"Stand still and let me lay hands on you. Because you are willing, it will not hurt."

Fann squared her shoulders and closed her eyes. The Morrigan laid her hands on Fann's shoulders.

"Try not to move."

A slow, creeping sensation crawled from behind her rib cage; it curled around her heart and wound into her bones. It washed up against her lungs, and she couldn't breathe—the Morrigan must be wrong—it was so deep within her—her crow-self, and she had had it always—how could she say goodbye?—had she made the wrong decision? But there was Slate, unmoving on the ground. And there was her life, here in the human world, already started. There was her *freedom*. And as she thought as much, the creeping sensation receded, and her lungs expanded, and she felt as if a great weight had been lifted from her insides. She thought to fly—no, dance!—with the lightness of it.

She bounced on the balls of her feet, a smile spreading.

"So it is as you wished," the Morrigan said softly.

"Hey," Slate said, struggling to sit up. "What happened?"

"Don't—don't get up," Fann said, leaping past the goddess. She knelt beside him and pushed gently on his chest. "Just wait till we make sure you're okay."

"I'm fine. I had the weirdest dream, though. Like I was in some kind of place for dead souls. Hell? I don't know. And you showed up." He looked at Fann. "I thought … I could fly."

Warm giddiness bubbled up in Fann's throat.

"Come here." He reached for her, pushing up again.

"Stop," she said, her hand still on his chest. "I'm coming." She leaned.

"Closer."

"I'm going to fall," she said, breathless, laughing, leaning over him, her face inches from his.

"I'll hold you up," he said, looking at her mouth, reaching for her neck.

The Morrigan cleared her throat. "All seems to be settled here. I will be on my way, then."

"No," Fann said. "I have questions."

"That is not generally how one requests an audience with a goddess, cheeky girl," the Morrigan said. "But I seem to be in the habit of making exceptions where you're concerned, so I suppose one more won't hurt."

"We'll give you your privacy," Leaf said.

"We're here if you need us," Slate whispered as she helped him stand, and then he followed the rest of the house members inside.

The Morrigan whirled at the Murder, raising a hand. "Murder be gone!"

The members of Fannilea Ishika Fiachra's former family leaned forward and dove as one. A great dark cloud swooped into the sky, rising above the house. Feathers blended, one into the other, and the tribe of uncanny crows flapped off, leaving behind the girl who was once their white-feathered crow-daughter. In her place they left a white-haired, blue-eyed human girl called Fann who thought she might explode with joy.

CHAPTER FIFTY-TWO

One last thing bothered Fann still. "I want to know who my mother is."

"Oh, come now. You've guessed."

"Yes," Fann said uncertainly. "I think … I think I saw it in your eyes."

"Don't be entertaining any softie-sweet ideas, there, girleen. The Morrigan is not the motherly type."

Fann snorted. "You think?"

"Besides, you are no longer of my people, which means we can have no ties."

"It's all right. I have a home, and a family. I just wanted to know."

"Now that you do, you might also appreciate the things your mother has done for you. They are a great many, do you know that?"

Fann eyeballed her, slantlike. "You mean like protecting Corley when I asked to see the Murder's feathers?"

"It is a delicate thing, the Murder. Upsetting the balance of it is also a delicate thing. Sometimes things must be … handled. In a certain way. And you … well, it is only just now that you've proven to me that you are *not*, in the slightest, a delicate thing."

Fann frowned. "You meant for it to happen, didn't you? All of it."

One corner of the witch's mouth crooked up. "I wouldn't say that. Even a goddess can only do so much. Especially with you in the mix. Ripping up the contract, that was … unexpected."

"You were testing me."

"You wanted to give up your Kaa self. That is not something you can take back. It is permanent. You will not hear from them again. You will not even know they exist. It will be as if you had a long, strange dream. I hope you do not have cause to regret your choice. Supposing I were the kind of goddess who allowed a Kaa to make that choice ... don't you think I'd need to be dead certain that it was what she really wanted?"

"Supposing you were," Fann said thoughtfully. "Did you let Azeel go?"

"Fann-girl, I am the Morrigan; I do not let people go." She paused, a secret smile threatening but not quite breaking. "But ... if you were to wonder who brought Azeel the makeberries that allowed him to live in the human world, you might find that a certain raven belonging to a certain goddess made rather a lot of trips back and forth between the Ahk and the human world during those times." The raven on her right shoulder hopped down and perched on her hand, and she smoothed the feathers on its head.

"I could not stop them from getting to Juanita," she said, eyes distant. "There was a war. I was distracted.

But when he returned ... perhaps he found me less difficult to fight than another might have. Perhaps he had an easier time plucking that tail feather than he might have. Perhaps it held a bit more magic than it might have.

"Afterward, perhaps the rules were ... tweaked. Such that now the Murder *must* call its goddess whenever there is a defector. So that she may ... intervene, if you will.

"Of course if you were to tell anyone that the Morrigan helped a Kaa to escape his Murder, no one would believe you. No one."

Her mouth fell grim, a hard straight line.

"Of course not," Fann said quickly. "Who would I tell?"

The Morrigan gazed into the distance, idly stroking the raven's feathers. "I suppose it's unavoidable. Every now and then, a Kaa is born who is constitutionally unfit to be Kaa. Who does not have shek in her blood after all."

"Who isn't a crow-sheep," Fann muttered.

The Morrigan bared her teeth.

"You may not believe it, Fann-girl, but the Murder you've dealt with is an afternoon tea party compared to what your predecessor Azeel came up against."

"Maybe I should do as Azeel did," Fann said, considering. "Tell my story, to make it easier for the next. Or … maybe it's not necessary."

The Morrigan's eyes narrowed. "What kind of poking-your-beak-in thoughts are you entertaining, Fann-girl?"

"What if … the rules were … tweaked again? What if … it's part of shek? If a member of the Murder chooses to escape the Ahk and remain in the human world, he or she must be let go." Fann pursed her lips. "You could make them bring her makeberries."

The Morrigan laughed. "The Murder is right—you are a tricksy sort. Like your mother." She sobered. "What about this: Any member of the Murder who escapes to the human world will have the option, if he or she so chooses, to remain in the human world permanently—if she agrees to become human permanently. Then she won't need makeberries."

"She won't be able to fly," Fann said wistfully.

"If she wants to be human, then she must be human."

"I know," Fann said, sighing. "But I am going to miss it. Sometimes."

"Do you regret?"

Fann shook her head. "Never. Tell me something, though. If you hadn't agreed, what would have happened to Slate? Would the makeberries have awoken him?"

"A goddess cannot reveal all her secrets, Fann-girl. You must be content with what is, rather than wondering about what might have been."

"I am. I just ... wondered. There's one more thing I have to ask. Slate's mother. She's been ..."

"I know how she's been," the Morrigan said sharply. "What of it?"

"I have an idea." She explained what she hoped for for Slate's mother.

The Morrigan eyed the white-haired girl. "Not afraid to ask a lot, are you?"

"She's almost there. You must know that she is. I don't think it's so much to ask."

The Morrigan sighed. "I don't suppose it is." She cackled. "And I have an idea of my own about who to send. Consider it done."

"Thank you."

"Well, then. All's well that ends well."

Fann studied her suspiciously. "How could you have known it would work out this way? You didn't know what any of us would do. You didn't know I would choose this house. To come across Slate, and his mother, and Azeel's story ..."

But then, why did she choose this house? She was reminded of when she had first landed. How she had seen the green of the garden, and then ... the white-feathered mask. The mask that had caught her eye, which now hung from a leftover nail on the wall in her bedroom.

"Is this yours?" Leaf had asked.

"You couldn't have known," Fann whispered.

The Morrigan cackled again. "Believe what you want, girleen. Whether I did or didn't know. It is none of your concern now. For the Morrigan is gone from you, up into the night, to return to her high—or low, depending on where you look from—post in the Otherworld, where she belongs, and you, my dear, do not, nevermore."

"Will I … will I see you?"

"If you do, you will not know. A knowing raven in your backyard? A strange woman peering at you in a café? A rather large black dog that follows you home? I have many forms. But fear not, Fann-girl. I will leave you to the life you asked for."

"That's not—"

"Hush now. I must go."

The Morrigan sashayed forward, and for a moment Fann thought she meant to kiss the top of her head, but instead she stretched out a hand and rested her fingers on Fann's forehead.

"Good luck, my once-daughter. I think you will do quite well without it, but I wish it for you all the same."

Before Fann could respond, the goddess transformed to her raven-self and exploded into the air. She flapped her wings mightily, cawed once, and flew off in the direction of the Ahk, her two raven pets by her side.

Fann held up a hand in a still wave. "Goodbye, Morrigan," she whispered. "And for whatever role you played, thank you. I think."

As she watched the Morrigan's form shrink to a black dot, tiny white bumps rose along Fann's arms and the back of her neck, and she shivered.

Her life was truly her own.

CHAPTER FIFTY-THREE

In the wee morning hours of the first day of the new year, a party raged at a certain half-built red-brick house with a rooftop garden.

There was food and drink, randomly collected though it may have been; music, eclectic and much argued about; and singing and dancing—some of which took place with reluctance (Scrap), some less so (Moonbeam and Jayda). There may have also been various strange and wild noises made, akin to hooting and hollering (Leaf and Fann), some flapping of arms in imitation of crows (Slate), and some recapping of what had happened earlier that night that was so exaggerated it didn't even come close to matching the truth (Scrap again).

Only two serious moments interrupted the festivities.

Fann pulled Scrap aside. "I have to ask you something. That thing you said to Corley, about having killed someone? Was it true?"

Scrap patted her arm, reminding her oddly of the Morrigan. "Fann, sweetie, this is a party! Topics of serious import should not be brought up. Besides, some things ought to stay buried for always."

Was that a wink he gave her?

Tilting her head, Fann thought that sometimes humans were just as tricksy as crows.

Later (or much earlier, depending on how one looked at it), when the noise-making and the singing and dancing had died down and the house members were beginning to yawn, Slate slipped his hand into

Fann's. He led her though the dining room and out the door, into the backyard, and she let him.

The night had turned chillier, and she could see her breath on the air, but next to her, Slate's warmth sent tiny thrills through her.

He stood close.

"We were interrupted, weren't we?" he said. "What were we doing? Something like this ...?"

He slid his hand up her forearm to her elbow, his iron-gray eyes sparkling, and he leaned in ...

This time, no one interrupted.

Epilogue

Time passes. Who can say how much? Crow-time does not pass the same way as human-time does. A few beats, or many. A few day-risings, or many. No one is counting.

Except, perhaps, the Morrigan, who makes sure it is not *too* many.

Somewhere in a large human city, not in the center but not fully outside of it, where a small row house with white siding and a dark red roof stands in front of a tiny square patch of yard, a large crow lands.

This crow has forward-turned shoulders, a barrel chest, and reedy legs, as well as two fire-bright eyes that sparkle with mischief and a careful empathy for the wicked. It perches on the chain-link fence next to the sprangled branches of the rose bush that tangle with it. Trapped in its beak is a small twig; from the twig hang three berries the color of blood.

The crow waits with patience, unmoving.

Out of the house comes a woman who once had a hush-soothe beauty, like a hot cup of tea. She locks the house-door and turns. There on the fence, the crow blinks at her. She approaches, and still it does not move. Instead it makes a low sound in its throat. She watches it with careful eyes, and it cocks its head, blinking more.

Three more steps and she stands before it. It shakes the berries. She stretches out her hand, and the crow opens its beak. The berries fall into the woman's palm. She cradles them there, her hands cupped and her dark brown eyes glistening.

The crow calls out a giant caw. It sounds like a reprimand. A scolding.

"I understand," the woman says. "It is done. I will grieve no more."

The crow watches her close, as though searching for Truth. Does he find it? Hard to say, for crows do not know of such things, do they? With one last pointy stare and a low throaty sound toward the woman's hand, the barrel-chested, reedy-legged crow leans forward and falls into the air.

As he flaps, rising, the woman tosses the berries into her mouth one by one, chewing them slowly. She eyeballs the crow as he flies, up and up until he turns to nothing but a black dot in the wide blue expanse above. She sucks the last of the berry juice off her teeth, and then she goes on her way. For now, she has things that must be done.

But tomorrow, she will call her son.

Rachael Ann Mare is a writer who never wanted to live for duty. She blogs about motivation and inspiration for creative people at SpunkyMisfitGirl.com. *The Flight of the White Crow* is her first novel.